David sat for a while in the burning silence beside Mr. Skinner's body and stared around him. He was still dazed, but the horror of the situation was leaping at him from all sides. Worst of all was the terrible feeling of loneliness—he was alive, he and Queen of Sheba, among all these dead. There was no one to turn to, no one to ask for help, no one to give directions. Skinner—his last faint hope—had died. Pa was gone—and Ma. He could only hope they were with the survivors, if there were any. If Pa lived through the raid, David knew he would eventually come back for his children. But if he was dead—

"Moeri has shaped this story with an unsensationalized precision that will compel readers through the experience of 12-year-old King David, who regains consciousness after the massacre of his wagon train and assumes responsibility for his little sister's life on a barren plain. . . . Vivid [and] memorable."

—*Booklist*, starred review

SAVE QUEEN OF SHEBA

SAVE QUEEN OF SHEBA

Louise Moeri

PUFFIN BOOKS

PUFFIN BOOKS
Published by the Penguin Group
Penguin Books USA Inc., 375 Hudson Street, New York, New York 10014, U.S.A.
Penguin Books Ltd, 27 Wrights Lane, London W8 5TZ, England
Penguin Books Australia Ltd, Ringwood, Victoria, Australia
Penguin Books Canada Ltd, 10 Alcorn Avenue, Toronto, Ontario, Canada M4V 3B2
Penguin Books (N.Z.) Ltd, 182-190 Wairau Road, Auckland 10, New Zealand

Penguin Books Ltd, Registered Offices: Harmondsworth, Middlesex, England

First published in the United States of America by E.P. Dutton, 1981
Published in Puffin Books, 1994

20 19 18 17 16 15 14 13 12 11

THE LIBRARY OF CONGRESS HAS CATALOGED THE DUTTON EDITION AS FOLLOWS:
Moeri, Louise.
Save Queen of Sheba.
Summary: After miraculously surviving a Sioux Indian raid on the trail to Oregon,
a brother and sister set out with few provisions to find the rest of the settlers.
[1. The West—Fiction. 2. Survival—Fiction.] I. Title.
PZ7.M7214Sav   1981   [Fic]   80-23019   ISBN 0-525-33202-2

Puffin Books ISBN 0-14-037148-6

Printed in the United States of America

1

A huge greenish black fly was crawling slowly over his hand. The fly was so close to his eyes, for his hand lay tossed up on the dirt just a few inches from his face, that King David could see every leg as it moved, the iridescent wings flick, the big bulbous eyes. He wondered why he did not move his hand and brush the fly away, but then a buzzing sounded in his head and his eyes closed and he seemed to sleep again.

The fly was still there. The buzzing in his head was softer, but now he was conscious of something else. There was a burning on the back of his neck as if he were lying facedown in the hot sun. Hot sun—yes, he was sure the sun was very hot. He was even sweating. Best to move to a shady spot, like under a tree. Why didn't he move to a shady spot?

The fly moved closer, boldly, not afraid. Another moment and it lifted into flight and landed on King David's face, his right cheek, just under his eye. He could feel the fly's sticky feet, feel its thirsty seeking for food, for blood—

Slowly, slowly the crawling feet of the fly stirred something way down deep in him. He felt muscles awaken as if from sleep, bones clack together. The hand before his face moved. And then he felt pain, and the pain made him catch a deep breath and cry out.

But the air he sucked in saved him, for it gave him strength to raise his head, get an arm under himself, pull himself up, look around.

Directly ahead lay a wagon, turned over on its side, and from beneath it protruded a man's leg. There was a man, then, under the wagon. Dizzily he turned his head to the right. There was a smashed keg which had held water, now soaked into the ground, and beside it another from which flour had spilled. Beyond that lay a horse, dead by the looks of him, and another man. There was an arrow sticking out of the man's back.

King David stared at the arrow and wondered if he too had an arrow in his back. Something hurt very bad but he could not tell what it was.

He turned and looked to the left. There were more kegs, boxes, some tools scattered here and there, and among them lay more people. All of them, men and women, one boy, lay in various positions as if somebody had raised them to a great height and dropped them, and they broke and died as they fell.

Slowly King David bent his knees and pulled his feet around to where he could see them. His gray hickory shirt was smeared with dirt and blood—more on the new black woolen britches his Ma had made for his twelfth birthday last week, and still more on his left arm where his head had lain. He raised a hand to his chest, his face, his head. Yes, there. High on his forehead was a ragged tear in the skin, and there seemed to be a loose flap of skin with hair on it hanging loose. He could tell there were thick, sticky clots of blood matted in his sandy hair and streaked down his sunburned, bony face.

"Tried to scalp me," he said aloud to the silence around him, "but didn't quite."

He could see that several wagons were scattered around—some of them had been burned, but the fires were out now, with only a heavy stinking smell of smoke that was drifting slowly away on the faint breeze. He now felt very thirsty, but it looked as if all the water kegs had been smashed, as well as sacks of flour and beans torn open and spilled on the ground. Slowly, carefully, he tried to stand up, but on the first attempt his head banged and roared and he had to stop. Then he crawled on hands and knees over to the nearest wagon, grasped the wheel in bloody hands, and pulled himself up.

Got to look around.

He felt fairly safe, oddly enough. He could see that the Sioux raiding party had gone. In the deathly silence the early afternoon sun beat down on the prairie and the wind washed idly over sightless faces turned up, over bloody clothing, quilts and household gear trampled into the earth. There was blood everywhere, on the bodies, on the ground. Besides the smoke, another curious, sickening smell was beginning to thicken in the hot air—a smell he would remember forever, the smell of death.

Carefully King David counted the wagons he could see. Five, six, seven wagons—four of them burned—lay scattered down the slight slope above the shallow draw, all overturned, their horses missing. Pa's wagon was not one of them. Pa—got away, he told himself in a rush of relief. But the relief was short-lived. Then—if he's all right—why didn't he come back for me? Pa and Ma—they must be hurt—maybe dying—or they'd have come back for me—

King David let go of the wagon wheel and started to walk, aimlessly, across the littered ground. His feet shuffled and his knees were weak, and he wished he had something to lean on. Something knocked against his ankle and he looked down. Without the slightest degree of surprise, he saw that it was a cane, still held in the clenched hand of a dead woman.

"Give—me—the—cane—Miz Stone—" he whispered. "I need it—"

He twisted the cane out of her stiffening fingers and, using it, began a slow circle of the wagons. It was very hard to think, but he began to piece some of it together. It must have been about eleven o'clock in the morning—Wagonmaster Keane, sitting tall on his big black horse at the head of the column, had just told them to halt for nooning, to eat a cold meal and to rest

4

and graze the stock. King David had been walking out ahead of the train, just behind Mr. Skinner, the guide, so as to get away from the dust raised by the wagons and the loose stock. This part of the train had been traveling on the Oregon Trail well south of the North Platte River and had crossed Scott's Bluffs by way of the Robidoux Pass. They had hoped, by taking this route, less heavily traveled now, to find better grass for the stock than they might have encountered on the trail that held close to the south bank of the North Platte.

After leaving Saint Louis, the settlers had disintegrated into several widely separated groups of wagons, with those pulled by horses—the "horse column"—far ahead of those pulled by oxen—the "cow column"— and King David knew that the wagons with ox teams were to go by the north fork of the trail that followed the Platte. By this time there was no telling where that part of the train would be, but he was sure they were too far away for him to be able to find them, especially since he was injured.

These seven wagons here had been slightly in the lead of their own small train, with a distance of a mile or so between them and the next group back, and their horses had already been unhitched. The remainder— the missing fourteen wagons with Pa's among them that lagged behind—were just coming into view, with horses, of course, still in the traces. Suddenly there had been a noise of yelling and trampling hooves, followed by shots and screaming. King David could remember the raiders—Sioux, somebody called them—coming out of the draws and gullies of the sand hills to their left.

It was too late to form a circle of wagons—the teams were already unhitched—and all the men could do was scramble for their guns while the women and children ran for cover. King David heard shouts, curses, shrieks, the sound of rifles, horses screaming. Then something struck his head—and like a curtain, darkness dropped over his memory.

So now he stared around. I'm alive, he told himself. These others here are all dead. And the rest of the wagons have gone on—escaped without me.

Suddenly he had a terrible need to find someone else alive. He had lived through the raid—surely someone else could have survived also. He stumbled from one body to the next, but only cold faces looked up, with blood splashed everywhere that was growing thick now, like red pudding cooked too long by the hot sun. Every once in a while the breeze stirred a shirt or a bonnet, and he thought for a moment that someone still lived, but each time when he went to see, he could hear no breath, no beat of a heart.

Past the farthest wagon lay a couple of wooden chairs, and under the chairs a feather bed. The breeze now freshening was lifting clots of feathers through holes in the ticking and tossing them up to drift idly away over the prairie. The white feathers looked like snowflakes, and in his thirst, the pressure of the heat of the sun, he was drawn to them, as if their cool whiteness could soothe the fever he could feel rising in him.

From under the feather bed a child's foot stuck out, shoeless, little, white. He looked at it for a moment but

6

did not expect it to move. His sister had little white feet . . . his sister, Queen of Sheba—

He sprang forward, jerked the feather bed back.

His sister lay quietly, looking up at him. "Are the Indians gone?" she whispered.

2

King David yanked the feather bed away from the child. She lay sprawled on her back, as if she had been pushed down suddenly, and her brown calico dress was smeared with dirt and blood. Beside her lay another body—a woman of about twenty years in a faded gray dress. The woman's breast was red with blood, and her face was set in a scream for all eternity—Letty Harmon, with whom Queen of Sheba was sometimes allowed to ride because Mrs. Harmon told her stories about fairies and elves.

For an instant King David was stunned to discover his sister's presence—her living presence—here among the dead. Then he grabbed the child and pulled her up thoughtlessly, not stopping to see if she was injured.

"Come on—git away from—there—Queen of Sheba—"

His sister clambered to her feet. There was dirt on her face and hands, and a white sunbonnet hung from her neck, the strings tangled in her long yellow hair. She had one shoe on and still held a gray knitted stocking in her right hand. Her blue eyes were vacant, her delicate face pale and dazed as she looked around.

"All—them—folks—" she whispered. "They're—hurt—"

"No," King David said quietly. "They're dead. At least everyone I've looked at is." He took a deep breath as he struggled to readjust his thinking. Only a few minutes ago he had been the only living soul here, and now there were two of them. But was it better or worse? Finding Queen of Sheba here was like finding a baby bird fallen from its nest—fragile, pulsing with life, but a life that would be so hard to save—

"Here—" King David struggled to pull himself together, to deal with what he had here instead of wasting time with wishing— "I got to find some place for you—"

He looked around for some kind of shelter for her, to remove her at least temporarily from the sight of violent death, and at last realized she would be best off in one of the wagons, if he could find one without any corpses in it. He led the way across the torn ground and, after inspecting two wagons, found one that contained only a pile of quilts and kitchenware. He pushed her into it.

"Stay in here, Queen of Sheba," he told her, "while I look—around. I got to see—if there's somebody else

9

alive besides us." Somebody—he told himself hopelessly—somebody who's *bigger* than I am—somebody who can tell me what to do—

Queen of Sheba sank like a frightened bird into the nest of quilts, and King David began a slow, careful tour of the shattered wagons. His head still ached, but he could think clearly now. There were twelve bodies scattered among the wreckage, and he was already sure that eleven of them were so mutilated there was no possibility of life remaining.

Of the twelfth—it was the guide, Luke Skinner—he could not be sure. Hope screamed through him as he examined the crumpled form. Oh, Lord, he prayed, let Mr. Skinner be alive. Even hurt, crippled—we could all make it together—somehow—

Luke Skinner lay on his face at a distance down a slight slope toward the shallow winding draw the wagons had been about to cross. He did not appear at first to be as badly wounded as the others. But as King David knelt beside him, ran trembling hands over the man's body, he found a little round hole in the buckskin coat—a bullet wound in the center of the back. It had not bled much, and King David, when he felt the old man's hand, thought he could feel a faint pulse. There seemed also to be the slightest puff of breath from the nostrils, and his flesh was warm.

King David tried to ease Mr. Skinner to a better position and see if he could help him, although it was clear to him even then that anyone shot in the back had almost no chance. He fought down an impulse to scream out and throw himself on the man's body. He

10

wanted to yell, "Don't die, Mr. Skinner! Don't die! Don't leave us all alone here!"

He found a basin near an overturned wagon and carried water from a muddy rain puddle in the nearby gully to bathe Mr. Skinner's face and hands and shaded him from the sun with a broken chair. But very soon King David could no longer feel the faint tick of the pulse, and a coolness began to spread through the body.

He sat for a while in the burning silence beside Mr. Skinner's body and stared around him. He was still dazed, but the horror of the situation was leaping at him from all sides. Worst of all was the terrible feeling of loneliness—he was alive, he and Queen of Sheba, among all these dead. There was no one to turn to, no one to ask for help, no one to give him directions. Skinner—his last faint hope—had died. Pa was gone—and Ma. He could only hope they were with the survivors, if there were any. If Pa lived through the raid, King David knew he would eventually come back for his children. But if he was dead—

After a while King David forced himself to get up and go back to the wagon where he had left Queen of Sheba. He decided he would not tell her about Mr. Skinner. She was only six years old—the less they talked about death the better it would be for her.

As he crept into the overturned wagon where he had left his sister, Queen of Sheba looked up. "King David, where is Ma? I want Ma."

King David had dreaded the moment when his sister would ask for their mother. Queen of Sheba was so little he knew she would cry for Ma and Pa. And what could he tell her? Only what he could make out so far. He eased himself down on a pile of quilts and rested his head that hurt so bad—so bad—

"Queen of Sheba, I'll tell you all I know. We been attacked. Sioux, I think, because I heard somebody yell that. You remember these wagons"—he gestured around them—"had stopped for nooning and the others were just coming up. I was walking ahead to git away from the dust, and Ma had let you ride with the Harmons for a while. Well—the way it looks, when the Indians hit us, the other wagons took off and managed to git away. I think from the tracks that the Indians was chasing them. So I guess maybe some of them might be wounded, too—" Or killed—

"But they'll come back for us—won't they?"

King David shut his eyes. He must be very careful how he thought and how he answered. If you let yourself hope for something that wasn't going to happen—you could just sit there and die, waiting and hoping.

"Queen of Sheba," he said at last, "we can't count on that. If Pa was able to come for us, he'd be here by now. So that means he's hurt." He did not say aloud the thing that was exploding inside his head: *or else he's dead.* "And if there are a lot of people hurt, maybe dying, in the other wagons, they'll have to run for it—try to make Fort Laramie. It looks to me like the Indians were still attacking them—the ones that got away—so they ain't got no choice but to run. No—they ain't coming back. If they was, they'd have been here by now. It's been"—he calculated rapidly—"three hours or more."

12

"Ma! I want my Ma!" Queen of Sheba's face began to crumple, and tears streaked down through the dirt on her face.

King David stared wearily at her. "She must be . . . with the rest of the wagons." Maybe hurt, maybe dead too, but I mustn't tell Queen of Sheba that.

Queen of Sheba, racked with sobs, clenched her arms around her knees. Her voice rose to a scream. "Ma! I want my Ma!"

The hairs on the back of King David's neck prickled. "Quiet!" he said sharply. "Hush up that noise, Queen of Sheba! Do you want to bring them Indians back?"

But nothing would stifle her grief except to cry it out, which she did at last. When she lay quietly, hiccuping a little, King David spoke again. "Queen of Sheba, I got to go out and look around. See what's left here— Maybe . . . we still got a chance. But we got to eat—we need a gun—"

He rose but then stood silent for a moment. He was listening to the echo of his own words. I talk like I had an idea what to do, he thought wonderingly to himself. I talk like I had a plan—like I was going to take hold here—

As Queen of Sheba stared wearily at him, he wiped one hand over his face, smearing the half-dried blood. Then he turned and slid through the torn canvas top of the wagon. He hated to leave the wagon, but the presence of his sister in the wreckage was like something pushing against him, forcing him to think, to move, whether he was ready or not.

Out of the fragile shelter, King David felt the horror of the scene strike him stronger than ever. Instead of

13

becoming accustomed to it, he felt the agony of those twisted bodies, the staring faces, worse with every passing moment. Death, if it had to come, ought to come quietly, like a tug at your sleeve, and not like a storm that swept everything before it—

He forced himself to make another slow, careful tour of the area, searching out anything he could find that would help them survive. At first he thought there was nothing at all, and then his eyes, sharpened by desperation, began to pick out an item here, another there. There were lots of quilts, a box of matches from the Harmon wagon, several pots and kettles. The Indians had destroyed or taken with them nearly every bite of food, but he found two good canteens, each containing a little water, one small sack of cornmeal almost full, and one little piece of bacon. There were some apples spilled from a barrel, and several were still good. He gathered them up and tied them into a bundle with a scrap of torn cloth. But the thing he needed most he could not find. A rifle. A gun of any kind. They *must* have a gun.

After a half hour of searching he sat down on the grass facing downslope. Mr. Skinner's body still lay there facedown with one arm crumpled beneath him. It looked as if Mr. Skinner had been running toward the draw—perhaps trying to escape—when he fell. Suddenly King David wondered what was in Mr. Skinner's hand—the one he could not see. After all, Mr. Skinner had managed to survive till the end of the raid—

He rose and wobbled down the slope. It took all his strength to turn the old man over. Sweat streamed down his face as he struggled to lift and turn him—

And there they were.

A Sharps rifle. A pouch of bullets. A box of caps in the old man's shirt pocket.

"Praise the Lord," whispered King David. "Praise the Lord."

3

Queen of Sheba sat in the shade of the torn wagon canvas, sullenly staring at the tin plate on her lap. "I won't eat it," she said.

"You got to. It's all we got."

"It's just old raw cornmeal. People don't eat cornmeal this way—Ma makes a pone out of it. Hot. To eat with beans."

Thinking with hungry, desperate longing of his mother's hot biscuits, her sausage and gravy, her bacon and eggs, King David scooped up a mouthful of the gritty meal and gulped it down with water from the puddle. It was like eating sand and washing it down with mud. "Eat it and hush up, Queen of Sheba. It's all I can find for now. And then you can have a nice apple."

"I want a piece of pone—some beans—"

"Oh, Lord." King David leaned back suddenly and shut his eyes for a moment. It ain't bad enough I'm half dead—I got Queen of Sheba too. I could—maybe—get out of this mess by myself. But how am I going to take care of me and her too? She's worse than a deadweight—I'll be lucky if she don't lay down in her tracks and I have to carry her—or else she'll run off on me. If only she'd been with Ma and Pa. Ma could always handle her. But . . . she wasn't. She's here. And they'll expect me to get her out too.

For a moment he let himself picture Ma and Pa, their lean, work-hardened hands and faces, their bodies stringy from struggle and hard times, the way they faced trouble like you'd face down a mad dog or a poison snake—fighting back with whatever you had at hand, and staying on your feet as long as you had breath and strength left. And that's what they'll expect of me. . . . He stared at Queen of Sheba, sitting dumpy and defiant with the plate of cornmeal untouched. I got to remember, he told himself, that she's only six years old and the baby of the family. She's not as strong as I was. When I was her age I had to carry wood and water, feed chickens, hoe corn.

"Queen of Sheba," he said carefully, "I'm too sick to cook anything, and I'd be afraid to start a fire if I could. Now, eat some cornmeal. We got to keep up our strength. After we eat—"

"Ma can fix me a corn pone. I want some nice hot pone." Queen of Sheba set her tin plate down on the ground and stared defiantly at him. King David clenched his fist and then let it fall. Queen of Sheba

17

was stubborn and willful—the more you pushed her, the harder she pushed back. Well, when she got hungry enough she'd eat raw cornmeal and like it.

"I want my shoe. King David, where's my shoe?"

Relieved, in a way, to face a lesser problem, King David looked at his sister's bare foot. She had a shoe and stocking on her right foot but none on the left, although she still had the other stocking, which she had stuffed into her pocket. No doubt when the raiders struck she had been sitting on a rock somewhere taking her shoes off—which she did constantly because she didn't like wearing shoes. Now, in the awful confusion of dead bodies and smashed wagons, he would have to search for and find her shoe.

"I'll see if I can find it," he said, handing her an apple. "Here—eat this."

King David took another apple and pushed himself up. Using Mrs. Stone's cane he began another round of the area. He was still very weak and had to stop every few minutes to rest. There were sharp stabbing pains in his head although the bleeding had stopped, and his knees felt like loose hinges that threatened to fold at every step.

Searching for a shoe was almost hopeless, he realized, as he turned over the scattered quilts, tools, and farm implements, bits and pieces of household gear. A horse could have trampled it into the dust or kicked it clear off into the deep grass. As he searched, he realized too that the sun was getting lower and the shadows lengthening. Before long it would be evening and then dark—and when night came King David wanted to be away from this awful place. He did not feel that

18

the Indians would return to the scene of the raid; more likely they would pursue the remnant of the wagon train and then withdraw to the north. But one thing he knew—he and Queen of Sheba had to get away from this place of death, for the living must not be entombed with the dead.

Shoe—a shoe. Where to find a shoe? Suddenly his eyes fell on the Harmon wagon. Mr. Harmon sometimes mended shoes for people— Maybe—?

He scrambled into the wagon and nearly fell over the body of Joseph Harmon. He jerked back, revulsed all over again, but then forced his eyes to take in every detail. Yes, there were two or three odd shoes—a man's heavy boot, a lady's smaller one, and—there—three or four little children's shoes. He grabbed up two that were a pair, made of smooth tan leather with black buttons up the sides, and crawled quickly over the body and out of the wagon, hurried back to Queen of Sheba.

"I think these will fit," he said as he knelt at his sister's feet, faintly grateful to have been so lucky. "But I didn't see no buttonhook. We'll have to button them without one."

Quickly he stripped off her own shoe and slipped on the new one, then the other stocking and the left shoe, and was fastening the buttons of the first when Queen of Sheba let out a bellow.

"Margaret Anne Beecham!" she screamed. "These are Margaret Anne Beecham's shoes! I won't wear Margaret Anne Beecham's shoes!" She bent over and started to rip them off.

King David rose to his feet. Completely without thought and almost without anger he brought the cane down on Queen of Sheba's hands. Stunned—hurt for the first time in her life—Queen of Sheba stared up at him.

"You wear them shoes, Queen of Sheba," said King David quietly, "or I'll beat you within an inch of your life."

The sun was very low and shadows were filling the hollows of the desolate sand hills. King David had gone from one body to another and closed the eyes of the dead. It seemed little enough to do for them—Pa would have dug graves and buried them, and Ma would have helped their families, comforted them, mothered lost children. Staring at the dead, King David felt an awful weariness come over him—what a useless death for people who had talked only a little of the hardships they left behind, but instead spun dreams of the future around the campfires every night.

Heber Stone and his wife had buried all of their children but one in Kentucky soil, where the tall trees choked out the corn and potatoes he planted on their small farm. Now Stone and his wife and that one son, Amos, lay here in arm's length of each other. Joe Pendergast was a harness maker but could never save enough to set himself up in business. The Harmons were a newly married couple who had no money to buy a farm. Their only hope had been to go west and settle on free land and make a future for themselves where hard work took the place of coin.

Besides Skinner, the guide, there was one single man, Peter Fleet, and two other couples, the Borers and the

Gradys, whom King David did not know well. Now none of them would ever reach the new country they had struggled to reach—Oregon—and their bones would bleach in the sun, their wagons rot, their horses and cattle would fatten the herds or fill the cooking pots of Sioux braves. King David suddenly knew, staring at the sightless faces, that his own Pa and Ma had known what this journey might cost. But they sold the extra stock, bought beans and rice and flour, shod the horses fresh, took their children and set out anyway. And now it was left to him . . . to finish this part of the great task, of the great journey. . . .

King David stood up and looked around, wondering urgently if he had missed anything that might help them. At his feet lay a pile of things he had gathered together for supplies. He knew he could not carry it all—Queen of Sheba would have to help a little—but he could only trust her with a small burden. He finally settled on letting her carry the apples he had earlier tied up in a bundle with a piece of cloth.

For himself there were a quilt, the rifle, the box of caps and the bullet pouch, a small piece of bacon wrapped in another scrap of cloth, a little tin box of matches, a sack of cornmeal, a knife the Indians had overlooked, the two partly full canteens, two coats that would fit them, and one very small tin pan. Leaving the cane because he felt it would be more burden than use, he made a pack out of the foodstuffs and coats in the quilt and bound it all together with a rope he found in one of the wagons. Not much equipment for two people making a journey across the wilderness.

Queen of Sheba picked up the bundle of apples. "It's

too heavy," she complained. Her knuckles were still red where King David had hit her, and her face was sullen. "I can't carry it."

"You got to," said King David. "You like apples, don't you? So you carry them and I'll carry the rest of the stuff."

"I don't want to carry apples. I want to ride in a wagon."

"There ain't no wagon. They're busted and the horses dead. We got to walk." King David took a deep breath; his lips were dry and parched, and his eyes felt like heated rocks set in his skull. He had wiped most of the blood from the wound off his face, but he could feel patches on his forehead and cheek where some of it had crusted and dried. He probably looked like a painted Indian himself, he thought, with the hair around the slash standing up in a stiff, crimson crest.

"Where we going?" asked Queen of Sheba as she set the bundle of apples down and rubbed her sore knuckles. Her face was mutinous.

King David absently scratched at the dried blood that was caked on his face. In the back of his mind the decision he would make had been forming and re-forming all afternoon, and now at last he felt he had sorted out the only course to take. They would have to follow the wagons, although he had already discovered that their tracks led away from the main wagon trail.

It was their own train, after all, that he must find. Pa's battered old Conestoga was not here. That meant that it—and Pa and Ma—were with the rest of the train. And the thing he wanted most in this world right now was to see Pa's face, hear his deep voice—feel the

22

crack of his hard fist as he growled, "Look alive, there, King David, look alive—"

"We only got one place to go, Queen of Sheba," he said at last. "We got to follow the rest of the wagons. Pa and Ma are with the wagons. We got to catch up with them."

Queen of Sheba scuffed a shoe on the ground. "I don't want to wear—"

King David made a threatening move.

Queen of Sheba fell silent.

"Come on. Pick up them apples—we got to git started. It's going to git dark pretty soon." King David wondered if his sister would raise a fuss at leaving the wagons, but she said nothing. He led the way down the slight slope, past Mr. Skinner's body, toward the bottom of the shallow gully that meandered northwards toward the sandy basin of the Platte River.

Suddenly his eyes fell on something he had not noticed before: Luke Skinner's hat. It was a broad-brimmed black felt, with a pheasant's tail feather stuck in the band. It lay near the feet of the old guide, and without much thought, or losing stride, King David grabbed it up as he walked by and slid the brim under the pack rope to hold it. A hat, he thought, was a good thing to have.

But as they walked away, leaving behind them the utter desolation of the overturned wagons, the abandoned dead, he turned for one last look. Shadows were long now, and in the coppery light of evening colored butterflies flitted in and out of torn wagon covers, beetles clacked through the crumpled grass, flies buzzed from one pool of dried blood to another.

23

I wish I could have buried them, said King David to himself, but I'm too weak. Can barely walk, take care of Queen of Sheba. He tried at last to think of a prayer to say before he left them. "Dear Lord, You take care of them. Forgive their sins. They was good people—"

Facing the wagons for the last time, he took in the sight that he knew he would carry with him for the rest of his days. "Lord," he said, "I don't never want to see no dead people again."

Then he turned and led Queen of Sheba toward the setting sun.

4

The sun sank below the horizon in sheets of orange and red light, and a pale transparent blue dusk settled over the prairie. The slight dips and rolls of the long reaches of grass, the sandy hills, began to fill with dark shadows, and a creek bed, which they had been following for the last half an hour, was darker still where clumps of cottonwoods and willows grew along the trickle of water. King David was grateful that the tracks of the wagons stayed close to the draw. Recent rains had kept the thread of water running in what in dry weather would have been a nearly dry gully, and good water was very scarce out here. The North Platte River was miles to the northwest, and in any case was so muddy that its water was hardly fit for cattle and horses, let alone man.

King David walked slowly, forcing each step. The pack was a leaden weight on his shoulders, and the rifle, loaded and ready to fire except for a cap, he carried muzzle down in his right hand. The box of caps was in his shirt pocket, and the bullet pouch hung on his shoulder. He hoped that he would be able to handle the balls and slip the caps into place fast enough to reload the gun if he should have to fire it. Besides the ever present threat of Indians, there were rattlesnakes, wolves, bandits—enough enemies to occupy an army.

The whole load of pack and rifle were so heavy he felt as if his legs would fold under him, but he had a burning need to put miles between them and the scene of the raid. Never before in his life had he seen violent death, and to be surrounded by it was more than he could bear. Queen of Sheba, being so much younger, seemed less disturbed by the dead bodies than she was by other things.

"Margaret Anne Beecham's shoes," Queen of Sheba muttered as she trailed him through the high grass. "I hate Margaret Anne Beecham. I don't want to wear her shoes."

"Be quiet."

"She's uppity. Just because her pa's got more money and better horses than our pa, she thinks she's better than me. I hate her. I won't wear her shoes—"

"Hush up, Queen of Sheba."

"I'm going to take them off right now—" Queen of Sheba plumped herself down and started to unbutton her left shoe.

King David forced himself to turn around, go back. "Queen of Sheba," he said flatly, "that's all you got to wear and you got to have something to protect your feet. I can't git you no other shoes now—I'll be lucky if I can keep us alive. When we catch up to the rest of the wagons—"

Queen of Sheba paused, looked up. "When are we going to catch up? I want *Ma*—"

"I don't—know. They're ahead of us someplace. We'll follow—tracks. But it'll take us a day or so—" He reached down with enormous effort and pulled her to her feet. "Come on—we got to hurry—"

"I'm cold."

King David loosened the pack and took out the smaller of the two coats he carried. "Here, put this on. We got to travel as far as we can—it's gittin dark—"

Queen of Sheba pulled the coat on and King David was glad she did not complain about it. For all he knew it might belong to Margaret Anne Beecham too, but he didn't think so. The Beecham wagon had not been among those that were left behind during the raid.

To keep his mind occupied, and out of a feeling that it would be all he could ever do for them, he set himself to remembering the names of the dead. There were Luke Skinner, and Mr. and Mrs. Heber Stone and their son, Amos. The Harmons, Joseph and Letty. Joe Pendergast. Another man with a red beard, whom he thought was Joe Pendergast's cousin or brother, named Peter Fleet. Then there were the two couples, the Borers and the Gradys, neither having any children. He must not forget any of them because he was the only one who would be able to tell the last chapter of their lives.

Most of all, as he plodded along through the deep-

27

ening dusk, he thought about the remaining wagons, and Pa and Ma, and how they would look when he and Queen of Sheba came into view—just a pinpoint on the horizon at first, and then closing the gap coming up, and how Pa and Ma would come running to meet them. He knew that he must not allow himself—even for a moment—to doubt that they would catch up with the wagons. Of course they would catch up. He must keep that picture in his mind, so that every step he took was just another step toward it.

"I'm tired." Queen of Sheba was lagging behind. "I want to rest."

King David halted. He tried to look around, but moving his head at all made it hurt so bad that lights danced in front of his eyes. Better find a place to stop, and quick, before he collapsed. "Come this way. We'll camp in the willows." He turned toward the creek bed, but even though it was only a few more yards, the scene was swaying before him by the time they got there.

Just under the lip of the high bank was a sizable clump of willows with several cottonwoods scattered through it. It made a fairly big grove, and King David sensed they would feel more sheltered there, whether in truth they were or not. Indians, if they were about, could probably find them anywhere.

They slid down the bank, crossed a narrow ribbon of damp sand, and then the slender branches of the willows gave easily before them as they found themselves beside a narrow thread of clear running water. Queen of Sheba for once was close behind, and he had a fleeting moment of being glad she was afraid of the dark.

At least she wouldn't wander off during the night.

King David paused for a moment to feel out a level place, clear of brush, where they could sleep. There was no hope of a fire or much to eat, but they could sleep at least.

Suddenly he froze. From directly ahead, almost in the stream bed, came a noise. Branches rustled and there was a stamping sound. Indians—on horseback?

"Stay here," he whispered to Queen of Sheba. "Right *here*. Don't move. I—got to see—"

Queen of Sheba, terrified at the noises in the brush, sank like a fawn beside the pack King David dropped. He slipped the knife out of his belt and crept forward, although he was so weak he doubted if he could strike a blow with it. The rifle was in his other hand.

Just ahead now he made out a huge bulky shape. But instead of being nearly silent as an Indian would have been, this person—or animal—was shifting and moving restlessly about. Now a smell tickled King David's nose—horse dung. A horse! Oh, Lord—he thought—it's a horse!

Feverishly he put the knife in his belt and crept forward. He had to get close enough to see what kind of a horse it was and why it was there— Why didn't it run away from him? An Indian's horse would take off like a frightened deer at the approach of a white man.

Carefully, carefully, one step at a time, King David went forward. He circled a little to the left and was relieved to see that he had escaped coming up behind the animal's heels. He had no wish to be kicked halfway back to Saint Louis by a nervous horse.

Now the animal began to take shape. It was a big

horse, blocky and heavy—too heavy to be an Indian pony. He reached out. "Ho, there. Ho, there." The horse snorted, its feet trampled nervously, but it did not bolt away. Something was holding it still.

King David's fingers, light as a feather, reached the warm, satin-smooth hide—a horse's neck. "Ho, there. Ho, there." Softly, gently, so as not to spook the horse, he moved closer, brushed his hand toward the animal's shoulder. Suddenly his fingers struck something smooth and hard. Leather. A leather horse collar!

King David let out the breath he had been holding. Oh, Lord! It was one of the horses from the wagon train, run away, no doubt, during the attack. Which horse it was he didn't know—it could have been any one of thirty. And still with the harness on.

It was caught somehow, probably by that very harness, here in the tangled grove of trees. He reached up and felt for a halter rope. Yes, here it was looped up over the hame. He untangled the rope, paid out its short length, and then wrapped and tied it around the trunk of a cottonwood tree. The horse was now tied, and he could be sure of it still being there when daylight came.

King David felt the ground under his back and realized dimly that he had fallen. Rather than get back to his feet, he simply turned over and crawled on hands and knees back to Queen of Sheba.

"It's a horse," he told her. "A horse. From one of the wagon teams. We—got—a chance, now—Queen of Sheba—we—got—a—chance—"

5

King David was awakened by a flock of birds that settled above them in the cottonwoods just before dawn. The sky, silver yellow in the east, was a clear deep blue overhead, with just a few wisps of fair-weather clouds that looked like feathers caught in the tops of the trees. Here in the ravine beside the trickle of water, the air was damp and cold and the ground under him felt wet, but just a few yards away on either side he could see the verge of the dry sand hills and beyond them lay the grass-grown prairie.

King David tried to sit up, but he could not get his head off the ground. His joints were stiff and every muscle ached from the hard ground, and when he moved his eyes a stab of pain went through them. He reached up and tried to feel the wound on his head, but his fingers were numb and he could only tell that there seemed to be a lump—a huge, swollen place—where the flap of skin and hair was. He felt feverish and weak.

Queen of Sheba was still asleep, lying on her back with the quilt he had put over her kicked back. A dry leaf had fallen and lay tangled in her yellow hair, and her dress was crumpled. She seemed to be all right now, but King David knew she was going to be hungry—and probably cranky—when she woke up.

There was a rattling sound over in the cottonwoods—a horse sneezing. Instantly, in spite of his wound and the weakness, King David rolled over. Dizzily he sat up and finally got to his feet. Got to get back to the horse—

The horse—a bay mare with a star-shaped blaze—was where he had left her, but she was restless and hungry. Now in the daylight he could see what had trapped her, holding her as securely as if someone had tied her there for him to find. The trunk of a broken sapling had slid neatly between the horse and the belly band of her harness.

She must have been moving slowly; otherwise the sharp pointed sapling could have slashed her belly. As it was, she had only a few scratches. In time she would have broken loose, and it was only their good luck that they had found her before she got away. Loose on the prairie they probably would never have seen her—certainly could not have caught her. King David muttered a short prayer of thanks as he broke the sapling off by stamping his foot across it (which made his head throb) and pulled it free of the harness.

By now the mare had pawed up a lot of dirt and eaten off all the grass and leaves she could reach. King David forced himself to creep around and pull armfuls of grass for her—she was a fair-sized horse and it would take plenty of feed to keep her.

The mare—he had recognized her by now as Heber Stone's horse, Maggie—turned her head toward the creek, her ears funneling forward eagerly. She wanted water, and he realized she had probably not had any since early yesterday.

Reluctantly he untied her and led her to the creek. She walked so fast she almost ran over him, and then plunged her velvet muzzle into the clear shallow water. He watched as the gulps of water traveled swiftly up her long throat. Presently she was satisfied, and she turned, chewing and slobbering, to dribble cold water over his hand and arm.

As he tied the mare back to her tree, he was very careful about the knot and seeing that she had enough grass to keep her quiet. He was beginning to realize that his condition was getting worse rather than better, and he couldn't afford to make the slightest mistake. He must take the greatest care not to lose the mare—she would make all the difference to them when they had so little with which to save themselves.

Queen of Sheba was awake and sitting up when he made his way back to her.

"I'm hungry," said his sister.

"I know. Eat some cornmeal."

"I want some hot mush."

"Ain't any. Eat—cornmeal—"

Queen of Sheba drew a deep breath and shrieked.

The noise crashed through his head. "That's—all—there is." he whispered. And then he lay down and it was like another night coming over him.

Queen of Sheba stared resentfully at King David. There he lay sleeping, his head on a fold of the quilt and one hand on the rifle, while she was hungry. King David had told her to eat gritty old cold cornmeal instead of making her some nice hot mush to eat with milk. King David was mean.

Automatically Queen of Sheba looked around to find Ma, so she could tell Ma how mean King David was. But all she could see were the clumps of willows and cottonwoods growing along the muddy stream bed and the awful endless canopy of blue sky overhead. There were birds flying up there, and Queen of Sheba stared at them till she got a crick in her neck, but the birds flew on and on and went out of sight at last.

And there was nothing else to look at anywhere—no high-wheeled jolting old wagon, no horses in jingling harness, no people bustling around starting breakfast over smoky campfires or hitching up horses for the day's trek. There was no great tall Pa to lift her up high in his arms and then press her close to his chest so that his beard tickled her cheek and she smelled tobacco and felt safe. No Ma to coax her to eat, to brush and braid her hair, to hold her on a warm lap when she was tired or frightened. No Ma. No Ma anywhere at all.

Tears blurred in her eyes, and for a few minutes Queen of Sheba felt them creeping down her cheeks like the little creek here beside them was creeping along across the prairie. But the tears seemed to wash something away from her, and after a while they stopped coming.

Then it was quiet and empty-feeling, as if something or someone had gone away. She watched King David for a while but he was just asleep, arms flung out, mouth a little open. A big blue black fly crawled around the wound in his head and he didn't even brush it away.

"King David?" she said, but he didn't answer. At last she got up and wandered off through the trees.

There were a few sunflowers blooming along the creek bed and she gathered a small bouquet. There were lots more birds and even some rabbits farther out on the prairie. After several minutes she found a nice shallow place in the stream where the water was as clear as a pane of glass and not much deeper, and she spent a long time making patties of good black mud and stacking them up like pancakes or biscuits, wiping her hands from time to time on her dress. Finally the mud pies made her think so much about eating that she went back to where King David was (still asleep) and ate some of the cornmeal. It didn't taste so bad this time, and she ate quite a bit. Then she was thirsty and drank some of the water from the stream. Satisfied, she wandered off again and found the mare, Maggie, tied to the tree.

The horse whinnied as Queen of Sheba came close to her, and snuffed eagerly. Queen of Sheba could see that King David had fed the horse some grass, but now nearly all of it was gone. Queen of Sheba stared at the horse. It was hungry, just like she had been. King

David ought to feed the horse. Pa always fed his horses—sometimes he even let Queen of Sheba hand wisps of hay to them or give them apples for a treat. At last, without much feeling or enthusiasm, she went and pulled several armloads of grass for the horse. For a while she watched the mare as she selected strands of grass with tender lips and then chewed and ground up the feed with her great strong yellow teeth, and the round balls of hay traveling up her throat to disappear into the depths of her belly.

When the sun reached the center of the sky, the heat and the silence made Queen of Sheba feel sleepy again. She turned and went back to where King David still lay, asleep on his back near the quilt. She stared at him for a moment. There was a swelling on his head just where the sandy hair started to grow, with an ugly red slash across it, and a green ooze was dripping out of the slash. His face was streaked with dirt, and from time to time he muttered words she could not understand. She watched King David for a few moments but he did not move. At last she too lay down. And just before she fell asleep, she wondered why Ma did not come and pick her up, lay her on a pallet of quilts in the back of the wagon. . . .

King David woke about sunset. There was a feeling of great alarm clanging through him, and he was very weak. He tried to sit up but couldn't make it. Queen of Sheba was sitting a few yards away eating cornmeal.

"There's green stuff coming out of your head," said Queen of Sheba, on seeing that he was awake.

King David raised a trembling hand and carefully felt his wound. It had swollen enormously, and he could feel something sticky seeping out of it. He swallowed. Infection. There had been a flap of loose skin yesterday, and now it was infected. Oh, Lord—that would be the end. With nothing to stop it, infection would grow and spread until it burned him up like a prairie fire.

He lay for a moment and tried to think what to do. Ma used to put poultices on wounds and soak them in hot water—but there was nothing like that out here. And once when a horse got an infected scratch on his leg, Pa had lanced it with his knife. All the green pus had run out, and then he and Pa had washed and washed the wound. The horse got better—in fact he was one of the horses that must at this minute be pulling their wagon. . . .

Slowly King David pulled the knife out of his belt. "Jesus, help me," he said softly. Lying flat on his back, he raised his left hand and felt the lump, steadied his right hand with the knife for one more moment. And then slashed—

Queen of Sheba screamed. She jumped to her feet. "King David—you cut off your head—"

Great stabs of pain shot through him, but after the first spurt of blood and pus, King David felt something else—a vast release of pressure and heat. He lay still for a few moments and then slowly rolled over. Pushing with everything he had in him, he dragged himself to the edge of the stream. He lowered his forehead into the water, tilting his face to keep his nose out of water, and felt the clean cold water rush into, through, out of the wound. He could see blood and pus drifting away on the current.

"Scalped—" he whispered. "Scalped. Pa won't— never believe—I did it myself—"

6

Several times during the night, a feeling of heat awoke King David. He had lain down on a patch of grass close to the deepest pool in the shallow stream, and each time the burning came, he roused himself and crept to the edge of the water. Tilting his face down, he let the cold clear water wash across the wound on his head. The slash was just about at the hairline, he felt dimly, but he had no way of knowing how large or how deep it was.

But each time he bathed it in the cold water, it seemed that he felt a little better a little longer. As dawn approached and the sky became gray in the east, he could feel the pain and swelling leaving him, and with that his mind seemed clearer too. He could feel the light morning wind on his face, hear the faint mur-

mur of the water only a few feet away, smell the damp earth and lush grass of the stream bed. And as he became aware of these things, he became aware of himself also, in a new and different way. I'm here—alive— me and Queen of Sheba, and all those others back there are dead. I wonder why we were the only ones. Why didn't some of the others make it? If even just one of them had lived—like Luke Skinner, maybe— what a difference it would have made. . . .

At last, tired of thinking about it, he put it out of his mind. Nobody, Luke Skinner or anybody else, was here to help him. Slowly, as if moving a heavy load, he turned over. Queen of Sheba lay asleep, wrapped in the old quilt, in the shelter of a twisted cottonwood tree. The bay mare was tethered downstream about thirty feet from where they lay, and as the light brightened, King David could see her stamping restlessly and her tail switching away flies. Got to get her some grass, he told himself, and soon. He hoped he would be able to get up and on his feet today—the mare must be cared for and kept in good shape. So far the mare— and the rifle—were the only lucky breaks they had had.

About sunrise, King David began to feel hungry. Leaving the rifle for the moment, he crawled over to the bag of cornmeal and forced himself to eat perhaps a cupful by dipping it into his palm and licking it up. It was so dry it nearly choked him, but then he crept back to the stream for a good long drink of water. What he wouldn't give, he thought after a moment's rest, for some of Ma's hot biscuits, her strong brown coffee, the beans she boiled with bacon and onions.

Thoughts of food—of cattle and wagons and armed

men—now pressed in on him, and as he lay back down beside the rifle he put his mind to work. He had by now forced himself to accept the fact that Pa and Ma both must have been hurt—and badly—during the raid, or they would have come back for him and Queen of Sheba. Nothing else would have made them abandon their children, whether those children were alive or dead.

But the train had taken an awful beating. The best, really, that he could hope for was that the missing wagons had escaped, though surely with much damage, and common sense told him that they would be certain to make for Fort Laramie with all the speed they could muster. By now they would be, at the very least, two days of travel ahead of him and Queen of Sheba.

Worst of all, King David could see that he would not be able to travel at all today. He had become very weak, and he had a choice of either holing up here and taking a chance on catching up with the train in a few days, or striking out before he had enough strength and dying for sure out there on the prairie. And that would leave Queen of Sheba utterly alone. . . .

The sun was well up when Queen of Sheba awoke. She opened her eyes and sat up, blinking around her at the arch of trees, the stream.

"Ma? Where is Ma?" she asked.

"Ma's in the wagon—they're—they're ahead of us." King David thought it best not to talk about their situation too much to Queen of Sheba. His sister was excitable and had a hot temper—best to keep her as quiet as he could.

"So what we're going to do," he went on, "is to camp here today—"

"I want *Ma*—"

"And then when I'm stronger we'll get on the horse and catch up with the wagons."

Queen of Sheba looked doubtfully at the bay mare. "She's a workhorse. She has a harness on, not a saddle."

"That don't matter. Lots of workhorses can be ridden. Why, I've seen Heber Stone ride this very horse lots of times—"

Truth was he had seen Stone ride *one* of his horses, but he couldn't really remember which one. He could only hope that this mare could be ridden, because he had grave doubts that either of them would have strength enough to cover the distance between them and the wagons on foot. He was injured; Queen of Sheba was only six years old. And the longer they lived on cornmeal and water, the less strength they would have.

Queen of Sheba ate a few mouthfuls of cornmeal and drank some water and then went off to make mud pies. Wish that's all *I* had to do, King David grunted to himself as he watched her become absorbed in her play. Then he wobbled off—half crawling and half walking—to see to the problem of feeding the mare. It would help if he had a long rope and could tether her where there was more grass, but the mare had only a bridle on with a halter under it, and a short halter rope.

Suddenly he remembered his pack. He had wrapped up the supplies he carried and tied them with a rope.

He crawled over to the clump of bushes where he had left the pack to see if the rope would be long enough for his needs. The pack was open and the rope lay carefully coiled nearby, although he did not recall having put it there.

With the rope in his hand he crept still on hands and knees toward the horse. He prayed she wouldn't spook at such a strange sight as he made.

The mare laid her ears back and snorted, but she stood until he got near. When he rose to his feet she let out a squeal, and he had to talk to her, soothe her, for several minutes before she would let him approach.

At last he went forward, untied the halter, and quickly tied the longer rope to the shorter one. Then he was able to move the mare to another tree which was surrounded by deep swales of good grass. She would feed there for hours. Gratefully King David crept back to the place where he had left Queen of Sheba and lay down to sleep.

It was late afternoon when he awoke. Flies were buzzing in the stillness, and he could hear meadowlarks singing as they skimmed through the hot air. A light breeze stirred the leaves of the willows and cottonwoods, and a few clouds drifted idly toward the horizon like sheep feeding in a vast blue pasture. King David took a deep breath and rolled over to look for Queen of Sheba.

But the glen was empty. Nothing moved except a few mosquitoes humming softly in the shadows under the willows. There was a big pile of mud pies, and some sticks and feathery grasses, a few wilted sunflow-

43

ers strewn here and there, but no little girl in a brown dress with tangled yellow hair and borrowed shoes.

Cursing the weakness in his legs, King David pushed himself up, called her name several times. There was no sound but the wind, the trickling water, the stamp of the horse dozing on her feet.

It was just like Queen of Sheba, he thought furiously, to wander off in the middle of Indian territory. No sense—no sense at all. Once again he cursed her presence here. Oh, God—if only she had been with Pa and Ma when the raiders struck. By himself he could eat, sleep, travel—survive somehow, get out of this awful mess. Having Queen of Sheba to look after was like having a broken arm or leg—the additional burden was likely to tip the balance against him just too far. But . . . what would he tell Pa . . . if he *did* make it back to the train—without her?

There was nothing to do but go and look for her. He picked up the rifle even though the weight of it was such a burden that he knew it would hold him back, but he did not dare lay it aside for more than a moment at a time. Looking both ways up and down the stream, he wondered tiredly which way to go. Since Queen Sheba liked to make mud pies so much he could only hope she had simply gone off to make more of them. Upstream or down? Then for no reason except that there was less brush that way, he turned upstream.

It took him several minutes to find her tracks, partly because his vision was still blurring out at times. In good health he could track fairly well—Pa had been teaching him, and he had picked up pointers listening to the old guide, Luke Skinner—but today his mind would not sort out the smudged marks; his attention was jerky. Mostly he was occupied with the fact that if Queen of Sheba had not been here, he could have put his whole strength into saving himself, instead of wasting what little he had looking for a disobedient child who like as not would only do this very thing again once he got her back.

He almost gave up twice, thinking he must have gone the wrong way, when finally he found a clear track in the black mud and, shortly after that, one of the high-buttoned shoes that Queen of Sheba had been wearing. Too tired to be grateful, he put the shoe inside his shirt. Grimly thinking that his sister deserved a good whack for taking it off, he then found the other. After being so lucky to have the shoes, he thought, all she does is keep taking them off.

With both shoes inside his shirt, he pressed on up the stream. By now it was near evening, and the sun was low in the sky. Its rays sparkled on the narrow leaves of the willows, making it even harder for him to see. He was on fire with mosquito bites, stupid with exhaustion, and his feet were wet from sloshing back and forth across the stream, but the thing that galled him almost more than the effort it cost him to search for Queen of Sheba was the knowledge that he wouldn't have the strength to spank her when he caught up with her. He thought longingly of willow switches and the welts he would like to raise on her legs.

Then as he slipped through a dense tangle of willows, he saw that the banks of the ravine had become higher, where flash floods had cut through a low rise, and before him spread a series of shallow pools fringed with tall grass and scrub willows. He blinked, caught his breath.

Queen of Sheba was sitting beside the nearest pool, cradling something he could not see in her arms. She looked up at him without surprise. "I got me a dolly," she told him calmly, as if she were seated on the front stoop of their old house in Missouri with King David coming in from doing the chores. She held up a short chunk of gnarled wood, and King David could indeed see that it resembled a human form, with a lump for a head and stubby arms and legs.

But he saw something else too. Something of vastly more importance than Queen of Sheba's doll.

Fifty feet beyond her on the crest of the bank was a rabbit. A big one. Maybe three or four pounds. Rabbit—

Carefully, silently, he eased the Sharps up, slipped a cap into place, sighted. "Don't move—" he whispered, "keep *quiet*—"

The rabbit's ears twitched—in a moment it would spring away.

The *crack!* of the rifle shot echoed across the draw, up against the flanks of the low hills. The rabbit squealed—sprang up—and rolled down the bank, dead.

7

King David squatted over the little pile of dry sticks and buffalo chips he had made under the cut bank of the draw. As he fed wisps of grass into the tiny blue flame beneath the fuel, he watched anxiously as a plume of smoke spiraled up and then drifted away on the breeze.

"Fan the smoke, Queen of Sheba," he said. "Don't let it go up straight—make it break up and blow away."

"I'm tired," crabbed Queen of Sheba. Her hand, waving a cluster of green branches, faltered. She still cradled the piece of twisted wood she called a doll in her other arm, patting and soothing it from time to time.

"You want to eat, don't you? You want to eat something besides raw cornmeal— All right, then, *help*—"

He had made the smallest fire possible and put the rabbit, skinned, cleaned, and cut up, in a little water in the small pan now balanced in the middle of the flames. Already the water was starting to boil, and the meat would be cooked enough to eat in a few minutes. And a few minutes, of course, was all he could possibly risk of a fire. The smell of smoke would drift a long way; if there were any Indians about, it wouldn't take them long to figure out where they were. There could even be an outside chance that the raiders who attacked the wagon train might double back this way. Either way, King David knew he did not have enough ammunition to stand any of them off for more than a few minutes.

But they had to have the meat. Raw cornmeal and apples would keep them from starving, maybe, but certainly not give them the strength they would need to cover the distance between them and the wagon train.

He poked the rabbit with a clean stick. "Lord, this smells good."

"I'm hungry." Queen of Sheba fanned the smoke listlessly.

She looked tired, dirty, lost. Ma would never have let her get mud on her dress, stickers in her hair. He wondered for a moment what Ma and Pa would say if they could see their children now—Queen of Sheba in borrowed shoes, her face sunburned under a layer of dirt, and him with a gaping wound in the crown of his head. Give them a turn, it would—

"I don't want to do this." Abruptly Queen of Sheba threw down the branches and walked away.

"Queen—dammit—"

Queen of Sheba's eyes bulged. "You *cussed!* I'm going to tell Ma—"

"Queen—you got to help me—I can't do it all by myself—come back and fan the smoke—please—"

Queen of Sheba drew herself up haughtily. "I don't got to do *nothing*. And I'm going to tell Ma you cussed—and that you hit me—"

"Oh, Lord," he muttered. "Oh, Lord—"

Queen of Sheba stamped away and flung herself down on a fallen log. She rubbed her dirty hands over her face, and after a moment King David could see that she was crying. "I'm hungry," she said softly. "I want Ma—"

Wearily King David stirred the fire and fed it a wisp of grass. It don't do no good to fight with her. I got to remember she's little, he told himself as he poured the water off the meat. I got to remember that she's little.

"Here," he said, forcing himself to be cheerful. "The rabbit is done. Lord, this is going to taste good. Come here, Queen of Sheba, I'll let you eat out of the pan."

For a few minutes they were silent as their fingers flew back and forth to their mouths. Queen of Sheba devoured her portion and picked the bones clean. King David noted her silence grimly—it was a good indication of how hungry she had been. When every scrap of the rabbit was gone, he selected an apple for each of them from the bundle. He even polished Queen of Sheba's apple briefly on his shirt sleeve.

The flames were gone now—King David could not

49

let the fire burn one extra minute—but there was a warm glow from the coals. Both of them crept close to the embers.

Queen of Sheba stared into the dying fire. Hunched against the gathering chill, she looked cold and little and defenseless. Behind her the shadows of the glade were dark and threatening, the willow trees only a fragile barrier between them and the dry, barren wilderness.

"Here, wrap this coat around you, Queen," said King David. "I got to let the fire die on account of it might be seen. But, Lord, it felt good while it lasted."

Queen of Sheba barely nodded.

Overhead the sky was darkening beyond the canopy of the trees, and the only sounds they could hear were the soft ripple of the stream, the first tentative hoots of an owl beginning his evening hunt, and crickets chirping in the heavy grass. Beyond the tiny circle of their camp—so barely furnished with a quilt, a few bites of food, the rifle, the knife—lay the prairie, the vast, silent, empty prairie.

For a moment, as his thoughts flew up like birds from this spot to range outward over the dark plain around them, King David was gripped by an awful tide of panic. Was he—a twelve-year-old boy, half dead already from the wound in his head—was he strong enough, smart enough, to overcome hunger and thirst, loneliness and distance, not to mention Queen of Sheba's foolishness, and take them forward over what unimaginable obstacles there might be to regain the safety of the wagon train?

But—I'm all there is. There's nobody but me, he told himself. Nobody. It's me or—

"Tell me a story."

King David looked up in surprise. He had thought Queen of Sheba was dozing. "Story?" he said blankly.

"Tell me a story. Ma always tells me a story at night." She stared confidently at him, as one who has only to ask and it shall be given. She looked like a frowsy little brown owl, perched on the fallen log with the wooden doll cradled in her lap.

"Ah . . . I can't think of a story—" King David searched his memory but, taken unaware, he couldn't recall a single tale to tell her.

Queen of Sheba began to cry. "Ma always tells me a story—"

"Oh—all right. Hush up. Be quiet—I'll—let's see—how about—how about the story of our names?"

"I heard that one before." Queen of Sheba huddled the wooden doll under her chin and rubbed her hand over her eyes. He could see she was very sleepy. If he could keep talking just another minute or two she would go to sleep, and then he could feed the horse, check her ropes, get some sleep himself.

"Well, it's all I can think of. Anyway—there was this big king called David, way back a long time ago," he began.

He sat hunched over, braced against the trunk of a cottonwood with the rifle across his knees, as he reached far back into memory of old days when Ma, knitting or sewing patchwork beside the fireplace after supper, had told them the history of their own beginnings. . . . "And this King David was a great soldier—"

"You was going to tell about *my* name—"

"I'm gittin to that. Well, this David killed Goliath—a very bad giant—and a whole bunch of other bad men. He had an army and he marched around the country making laws and telling the people to do right. At last he got to be king there in Jerusalem—"

Queen of Sheba yawned.

"And everybody heard how great he was. And he wrote songs—we call them psalms—and when I was born, Pa said he wanted to name me after him because he was strong in battle for the Lord."

"Tell about Sheba." His sister's eyes were heavy and she was nodding.

"Well, David, he had a son called Solomon, and Solomon was a great king too. Well, not as great as David—"

Queen of Sheba's face darkened.

"But he was a pretty great king—" King David conceded grudgingly. "In fact he was so great that people heard about him in other countries far away. And there was a great—*great*—queen of a country called Sheba, and she wanted to know if Solomon was as wonderful as she had heard he was. So she loaded up all her servants and her gold and treasures on her camels and elephants, and she made a long journey. She went all the way to Jerusalem to see Solomon. And when she got there she gave Solomon lots of presents, and he gave *her* lots of presents—"

"Gold?" asked Queen of Sheba sleepily. "Jewels?"

"Yeah, all of them things. And then the Queen of

Sheba went home to her own country. And so when you were born"—he did not tell her that two other babies had been born and died before her—"Ma and Pa thought you was really something wonderful. So they called you Queen of Sheba because she was a great lady, and they want you to be a great lady too—"

Queen of Sheba sank quietly down on the leafy ground. "I'm . . . going to . . . be a . . . great lady," she whispered as she fell asleep.

King David took the quilt and tucked it around her, scraped dirt over the coals to cover the fire. As he took up the rifle to make a round of the grove and the camp, and feed the horse, he looked down. "Yeah. You'll be a great lady someday—if I can keep you alive."

8

Day dawned brassy and unusually warm. King David woke sweating, and when he struggled to sit up, he could see there was a heavy dew on the grass.

For several moments he sat staring around at the shaded dell beside the creek. He felt nervous, almost afraid, as if he had been awakened by a noise of something dangerous, and yet he could see nothing to cause immediate alarm. Downstream a few yards the bay mare, Maggie, dozed on her feet, her tail switching off a few early flies. Queen of Sheba still slept, wrapped in the quilt. The remains of the little fire were long since only blackened coals, and he had buried the bones of the rabbit so as to keep any wandering coyotes or wolves from smelling them and venturing too near the camp.

He raised a hand and very carefully felt the wound in his head. He was vastly relieved to feel the swelling less and no wet ooze seeping out of it, but he wondered what it looked like—it gave him an uneasy feeling that there was this gaping hole in the scalp and hair that ought to cover his skull. A person hadn't ought to be walking around with broad daylight shining down into his brains. . . .

After a few moments of fruitlessly thinking about his wound, he crept quietly over to the sack of cornmeal and ate several mouthfuls, washing them down with water dipped up from the creek in his palm. On his feet at last, he stretched, tried out a good walking stride. He was still shaky, but enormously improved over yesterday. Take more to kill me, he told himself grimly, than a Sioux knife.

He untied the mare and took her to the stream to drink and then, with the rifle close at hand, gathered bunches of grass for her. Maggie tossed the sweet grass with her nose and then settled to a comfortable munching. King David stood silent for a moment beside the mare. He had never taken her harness off, and she was probably pretty tired of it by now. He ran his hands in under the collar but could find no raw places where it was wearing on her tough hide, and no stickers or ticks. Of all things that could happen to them now, loss of the horse would hit them hardest, next to losing the rifle. Maggie, he assured himself, looked fit. Time to get ready—get started—

He waked Queen of Sheba and bade her eat some cornmeal. Queen of Sheba was cranky.

"I don't want cornmeal. I want some hot mush, with milk on."

"Ain't got any."

"Where's Ma? I want my Ma."

"She's—that's what we're going to do today, Queen of Sheba. We're going to start catching up with the wagons—with Ma and Pa."

Queen of Sheba sat up. "We're going to find Ma today?"

"Well—" He wondered how much to promise her. Queen of Sheba was old enough to remember what he said and to hold him to it. "We're going to *start* today. I don't reckon we'll catch up for three, maybe four or five days. It depends on how fast we can travel."

He knew they had lost a serious amount of time. The wagons would have traveled, probably at a gallop, for a short distance during the actual attack. More than likely then they would have rested a short while to let the horses blow and then struggled on. Wagonmaster Keane (if he was still alive) would press them hard as he could to put as much distance behind them as possible, for every mile they passed brought them nearer to Fort Laramie and safety.

Trouble was, King David did not know how far he and Queen of Sheba were from the fort, nor exactly where it lay. Fortunately he had paid close attention when the men of the train were talking among themselves, and had automatically memorized everything he had heard about landmarks and the trail between here and Fort Laramie. The land would be rising gradually out of the endless prairie, and there would be bluffs and outcroppings of rock, ravines, and more sand hills.

The wagon train had already sighted Chimney Rock a couple of days before the raid and had camped at Robidoux Pass in the Scott's Bluff country the night before the Indian attack. One branch of the main wagon trail followed directly from there along the south bank of the North Platte River, but the wagons of their own train had taken the other branch of the trail farther to the south, and now they had even veered to the south of that trail—probably cut off by the Indians. And King David felt that he had to follow the wagons of his own party rather than turn north to the main trail. If they could make good enough time they should be able to catch up, because a wagon train seldom made much more than fifteen miles a day. Finding the horse had made all the difference in the world to them; by taking turns riding her, their chances of either catching up or at least making it to the fort before they got so hungry they could no longer travel were a hundred times better.

King David was not too worried about finding their way—following the wagons—across the empty land. All he had to do was stay with the tracks of horses and wagons, and a half-blind man could do that. He was worried about Indians, about food, about water, but not about following the trail. Fourteen wagons and a herd of loose cattle and horses would leave a trail that even a boy like himself could follow.

The sun was climbing, glinting in his eyes. Time to go.

King David untied the mare and brought her back to the little camp. He rolled the pack and fastened it across the mare's back by lashing it to her harness.

Maggie turned her head and snuffed the pack, but made no real effort to dislodge it, though once or twice she raised a hind foot as if she would kick him if he got behind her. King David was careful to stay where she could not land a blow with those huge hammers, and he wished he had more time to try the mare out, see how gentle she was before he trusted her to carry Queen of Sheba. But he had only so much strength, and even less time.

"Come here, Queen." He grabbed his sister and lifted her with one convulsive surge of energy that left him gasping, but got her onto the horse. Queen of Sheba's eyes bulged and her free hand clenched the right hame; her left arm was wrapped around her doll.

For one moment both of them were silent while they waited to see what Maggie would do. Then Maggie's head went down, and King David thought she was going to buck. He seized the bridle and pulled her sharply around. Maggie, distracted, laid her ears back but seemed unable to concentrate on her aggravation. She snorted, coughed, bared her teeth, but didn't buck.

King David let out a tightly held breath. He picked up the rifle in his right hand, took the halter rope in his left, and led Maggie up out of the creek bed, turned toward the west.

They were on their way.

9

"King David—it's the valley of the dry bones!"

King David, still leading the mare while Queen of Sheba rode, yanked her to a halt and stared around. They had just crossed a saddle between two low hills and entered a small vale of perhaps a third of a mile square. Before them on every side lay clumps and clusters of bleached bones—great arching ribs, convoluted vertebrae, thick and heavy leg bones, huge skulls with horns still attached. Tufts of dry grass and prickly pears laden with sharp spears glistened through the ivory thickets, and lizards darted here and there almost too fast to see.

"I don't know—what it is—" King David stumbled as his foot collided with one of the skulls. "I ain't never seen—so many—"

Queen of Sheba leaned forward fearfully. "Are they people's bones?"

King David's eyes raked over the bones nearest him. "Oh—of course not!" he said impatiently. "They're too big to be people's bones. And people don't have horns." He raised his foot and tried to kick the skull out of the way, but it was too heavy for him even to move.

"Look at them, Queen of Sheba, they're buffalo. People don't have skulls like that—or horns—or ribs that big around—"

Queen of Sheba looked doubtful. "I don't know what kind of ribs people have. I never seen any. I think this is the valley of the dry bones like it tells about in the Bible."

King David shaded his eyes and tried to make a rough count of the skeletons but quit after he reached thirty-nine. The sun glancing off the stark white surfaces of bone made splinters of light that pained him, and the wind streaming through the rib cages whistled eerily in his ears.

Behind him, Maggie snorted nervously, raising first one hind foot and then the other as if to kick. She could still scent death even now when the blood, the torn flesh, the stink of corruption were long since burned away from the slaughtered buffalo carcasses by the prairie sun. King David glanced over his shoulder, wondering if he would be able to lead the mare across the vale or if they would have to go around. Maggie was jumpy as a hare and could easily snap the rope out of his hand and charge off across country if she took the notion. But he hated the idea of turning aside—

every step added to their journey made the outcome more doubtful.

"Queen of Sheba," he said, "maybe you better git off and walk while we go across here. Maggie's liable to act up and you might git thrown off."

Queen of Sheba shivered. "I ain't going to walk through them dry bones," she said flatly. "They going to rise up and live again."

"Oh—stop that—" said King David irritably. "This ain't the valley of the dry bones where the Lord raised dead people up and put muscles and skin on them. That was in—well, someplace over in—Jerusalem, I think. Anyway, a long way from here. And these ain't *people*—they're buffalo—"

"How do you know? You ain't never seen dead buffalo before."

"But I can see—oh, what's the use? Stay on the horse then. Hang on. And if she starts to buck, jump off quick. I got to hang onto the rope and I might not be able to catch you."

King David jerked the rope but Maggie seemed to have turned to stone, immovable. He jerked again and her ears flattened. Queen of Sheba watched the horse uneasily and peered down at the ground.

"I don't want to fall down on them dry bones," she muttered. "They going to rise—again—"

"Oh, forget about them! You ain't got the sense the Lord give a goose! They're just old buffalo bones—" King David got a better grip on the halter rope and hauled hard on it as Maggie leaned backwards, her legs like four heavy tree trunks rooted in the earth. Her eyes were beginning to roll.

"I know what it is—now—" panted King David. "Buffalo—killed—here—by hide hunters— Pa told me about them—"

He stopped pulling on the halter rope to catch his breath. The slightest extra effort exhausted him. Maybe if he let the mare stand for a few more minutes she would calm down. Otherwise they would have to make a detour around the area, adding almost another mile to their already endless odyssey.

Queen of Sheba folded her arms. "If they're buffalo, why would somebody kill all this many in one place? They couldn't nobody eat this many buffaloes at once."

King David eyed the horse. She seemed steadier now, and he sank to one knee, resting the stock of the heavy Sharps on the ground beside him.

"I told you," he said absently. "They been shot by hide hunters. Hide hunters just kill all the buffalo they can and take the skins off and leave the carcasses to rot. They don't eat the meat—they just take the skins."

"What for?" asked Queen of Sheba doubtfully.

"To be sold. Tanned for buffalo robes. To make leather, maybe, I don't know. I guess they make money that way."

Maggie lowered her head and her velvet muzzle dusted lightly over the huge skull that lay near them. King David could see a shiver of fear that rippled over her like water rippling when the wind blows. He hoped she would sense that the skull, the bones, held no threat for them.

"I don't believe you," said Queen of Sheba. "Mr. Skinner killed a buffalo for us once and all the families got some of the meat and it was good to eat. . . . I'm hungry."

"Yeah. Of course it's good meat. That's why the Indians hunt buffalo."

"Maybe the Indians ate these."

"No—it's hide hunters did this. Indians couldn't have killed this many all together out in the open, and they would have carried lots of pieces away to cook and make jerky of. That way, lots of the bones would be missing now. No—nobody ate this meat. It just laid here and rotted and was wasted."

The hot wind blowing across the vale made no noise, and King David could hear his own voice as loud as if it were a thunderclap. The wind had no smell either, but he could imagine the terrible stench that must have filled this part of the prairie long ago, when the mighty beasts were killed and left to putrefy in the hot sun. The Indians must have been able to smell it from miles away. And knew as they drew the odor into their nostrils that the flesh of those slaughtered beasts would never boil into savory stew to feed them, their children, their old folks. Sioux bellies must have growled with hunger at that smell—the stink was probably still with them as they sighted down their arrow shafts at white faces—at white men who killed for hides, for fur, and left good meat to rot. . . .

Maggie raised her head. She seemed to be satisfied that the skull would not attack her. King David crawled to his feet, picking up the rifle.

"I'm going to try and lead her across," he said. "Hang on tight."

63

Queen of Sheba gripped the hames and her eyes rolled nervously from side to side as King David jerked the halter rope and started forward. Maggie snorted and balked but at last took one reluctant step, another, another.

Down in the swale, the sense of death was even stronger. King David found himself glancing left and right, back over his shoulders, as he guided the mare between the piles of bones.

Suddenly Queen of Sheba let out a squeal. "Look! See—I told you—them bones over there are going to rise—"

King David snapped around to look where she was pointing. There indeed was a pile of bones that stirred, rustled, *rattled*—

"Oh—hell—Queen of Sheba—that's only a snake—a rattler—inside a bunch of bones—" Even at this distance, King David could clearly see the writhing brown and gray length of the huge prairie rattler as it lay coiled to strike. Its tail was a blur but he could hear the fierce staccato warning of danger—of death—

Maggie's head snapped up, straining the halter rope to the utmost. Her eyes showed white and her feet began to dance as she threw herself to the right, away from the snake.

"Shoot it!" cried Queen of Sheba.

"What for?" King David fought to keep his hold on the rope as his feet dug furrows in the dirt. "It's a snake—he ain't going to hurt us that far away—and I can't waste a bullet—"

"Kill it! Kill it!"

"No." They were past the snake now and picking

64

their way up the next slope. Maggie swung her head to look back, snorting, and Queen of Sheba's face was wild.

"Why don't you kill it?" she cried.

"What's the use? It's like killing flies—a hundred more would come to the funeral. And we didn't git hurt. Anyway—there's been enough—killing—out here."

When they topped the rim of the swale, they halted. Panting, King David mopped the sweat from his eyes. As they looked back over the silent field of death, the pile of bones that hid the snake settled with a soft clacking sound into a different shape as the reptile crawled away. Now the row of ribs stabbed up at the sky like the fingers of a dying man.

"See?" muttered Queen of Sheba. "I was right. I told you—these bones would rise—"

It took him until late in the morning to locate the main track of the wagons. It appeared that, in the confusion after the raid, the wagons of a few of the survivors had been separated from the rest, and it took him several wide passes to find the place where he felt they had all assembled again. The sun was in the noon position when he stood on the crest of a low rise and squinted ahead to where a broad path of wheel tracks, tumbled rocks, and crushed grass marked the trail.

"Where is Ma and Pa, King David? I want to catch up with Ma." Queen of Sheba, perched on Maggie's broad back with one hand gripping the hame for balance and the other clutching her doll, wriggled restlessly. "I don't know why Pa called you King David.

You can't even find Pa and Ma and the wagon. You don't look like no king to me."

King David glared weakly at his sister. "All right," he said, "don't call me King David no more. From now on you can't talk to me at all unless you call me by my middle name—Anaximander."

That'll hold her, he told himself. That old Greek fellow's name that I heard about in school once—that'll hold her for a while. King David was surprised and pleased at his own ingenuity in devising a plan of such bloodless cruelty. Telling Queen of Sheba that she couldn't rave at him was meaner than hitting her, and wouldn't even leave a bruise that Pa and Ma would hold him to account for. He grinned.

"A—man—"

"No."

"Anka—"

"No. Don't talk to me less you can say it right."

"Anka—salanka—" Queen of Sheba's voice slid up to an eerie howl. "—sander—"

She took a deep breath and began to bawl. For such a little girl she could emit an unbelievable volume of sound. The empty prairie seemed to fill up with it. Maggie's head began to sink and she bowed her back. Visions of a bucking horse rose before King David. He wasn't ready for that.

"Oh—keep quiet!" he bellowed. "Never mind—you can call me King David—just—keep quiet!"

Queen of Sheba subsided into a wheezy blubber. "And I don't like to ride this horse, neither."

"You sure are brave and cheerful, Queen of Sheba," said King David furiously. "A real pilgrim. But you

66

ain't big enough to walk all the way we got to go. So just sit there and ride—and keep quiet. Don't do nothing to spook the horse."

Directly ahead lay a clump of prickly pear cactus and King David steered the mare around it. Maggie took a lot of watching—she was skittish about badger holes, startled easily if a bird flew up near her, and she stumbled over every rock. King David was glad Pa had taught him a good deal about handling fractious horses. Now, after traveling for several hours with Maggie, he felt he had learned quite a lot more. . . .

"Which way we going?" asked Queen of Sheba impatiently.

"Straight ahead. Follow those tracks. Easy."

But late in the afternoon he began to wonder just how easy it was going to be. A chill breeze sprang up, and in a few minutes heavy thunderheads began to build on the horizon and then raced toward them. In a remarkably short time the sun winked out behind the pewter gray clouds, and soon after that they felt the first raindrops.

"Just a shower," King David muttered, buttoning on the bigger of the two coats and handing the smaller one to Queen of Sheba. He took Luke Skinner's hat from under the pack rope. "Don't want the rain to run into my head," he muttered as he gingerly settled it low over his eyes. "Might git some tadpoles in it."

He was faintly sorry for having made her bawl—Pa would have walloped him for teasing her—but Queen of Sheba, huddled on Maggie's back like a sparrow on a rail fence, stared blankly at him and did not even smile at his feeble joke. King David thought about making an ugly face at her but decided it wasn't worth it. Winding the halter rope around his fist, he kicked Maggie in the belly to urge her on.

The storm grew heavier as the moments passed, and the prairie, seen through a curtain of rain, began to look watery and indistinct. Thunder crashed in their ears till they felt bruised, and lightning forked down on all sides. The nervous mare snorted and rolled her eyes and Queen of Sheba screamed. A raging wind now arose and drove the rain straight into their faces like silver nails. The borrowed coats started to leak, and water seeped down their necks. Queen of Sheba began to cry again.

Shivering, drenched, blinded by the rain, King David plodded forward, dragging the mare behind him as the water soaked into her collar pad and made wet mops out of her black mane and tail. He tried to look up, search out the trail, but soon realized that his eyes were no match for the storm. All the grass was flattened now—gouts of water filled every hollow, sheeted from every rise. What he thought were tracks could have been anything, and in a very short time he realized that he had lost the trail.

A stab of lightning struck the earth ahead and to the left, and its thunderbolt crashed in their ears. King David staggered, but in the single instant of illumination he had seen a low bluff directly ahead—a small rise with tumbled rocky walls. Surely there would be an overhang of rock there—something to break the awful force of the storm.

Stumbling, struggling, cursing, King David dragged

the frenzied mare up the short slope. Ahead were the rocks—there—there—an overhang!

Oh, Lord—he breathed as he hauled the mare into the shelter behind a jumbled toss of huge boulders—thanks, Lord, we couldn't have made it much further—"

10

The rifle, the horse, and now a shelter. Once again they had found help—not much, but enough to keep them alive.

There was a fair-sized cave behind the overhang; and as King David felt his way back into its depths, he could see that it had sheltered many—both men and beasts. There was a litter of small bones—probably rabbits and birds—and some larger ones that looked like antelope or deer. There was even a place where the blackened stone overhead showed that fires had been built here. A few sticks and some buffalo chips that someone had brought and left still lay about, and King David thought longingly of a fire. It would have to be carefully done though, because even though the fire would not show past the mouth of the cave, the smell of smoke could drift a long way on the wind.

He reached up for Queen of Sheba, and she was so tired she simply turned and rolled off the horse into his arms. His knees buckled under her weight before he could ease her to the ground. Then he led the horse to the back of the shelter where he could tether her to some rocks. The mare lowered her head to snort at the bones, but she was too tired to raise a proper fuss. She kicked irritably; she was probably itching and galled from wearing her harness for so many hours. He would take it off now for a while and try to dry the leather, but first he had to see how safe they were.

"You can sit here with your doll," he told Queen of Sheba as he untied the pack and laid it beside the fire pit. Queen of Sheba sank into a wet, huddled lump, still holding the knobby piece of wood in her arms. "I'll tie the horse up and go take a look around." King David took the rope off the hame and tied one end to Maggie's bridle, paid out a short length, and fastened it as tight as he could around a boulder on the cave floor. Maggie let out a long rattling sigh and snorted up dust from the floor, then quickly fell into a doze, resting one hind foot on the rim. Beads of rainwater dripped off her harness and the longest hairs in her mane and tail.

Rifle in hand, King David returned to the opening of the cave. The rain was still falling in a blinding downpour, but he wanted to have a clearer idea of where they were. He glanced back. Queen of Sheba sat where he had dropped her. Her head was bent and

71

she seemed absorbed in her doll. He had a moment of mild gratitude that she had found the doll—it might keep her from plaguing him so much. Queen of Sheba was fierce about seizing on something and not letting go—only last winter she had bawled bloody murder when a pretty icicle she had brought into the cabin melted from the heat of the fire. Ma had to give her barley sugar to shut her up. . . .

Rifle in hand, King David slipped out past the boulders at the mouth of the cave. As he climbed the last steep pitch of the slope, clambered through a slot in the rimrock, and came out on top of the mesa, he could see that it was larger than he had thought—maybe more than a quarter of a mile long in all. The top was flat and grassy and the upper sides nothing but crumbling reddish gray rock, with the steeply slanting slopes leading down to the flatter land on all sides.

As far as he could see lay only more broken country, and far off to one side a blur of dark blue that might be mountains. He was fairly sure that direction was west. Before the rain started he had depended on the sun's position for directions, although he hardly needed even that as long as he had the trail of the wagons to follow, which had swung back to a rough northwesterly course. Now the rain, in addition to blotting out sun and stars, would no doubt raise havoc with the trail too, soaking and blurring it, but there was nothing to be done now but to wait it out. When the rain quit he would have to find the trail again—what was left of it—a matter of circling the butte till he cut across the tracks. Pa would probably have been able to track right through the rain, without having to crawl into a cave to wait it out. For a moment he thought hungrily of how good it would be to have Pa up ahead of him again, to see Pa's broad back and his lean brown face—always sober and often frowning—turned like a wedge this way or that so King David knew which direction to take—

With the rain pelting his face, he searched the horizon for a long time but could see nothing but rolling grassland with occasional breaks like the one they were on. There were, of course, no signs of another human being anywhere. At last he turned to go back to the cave. On the way he pulled up a huge armful of grass—all he could carry—for the mare. Got to feed her, got to keep her strong. Take her harness off, rub her down.

Once the mare had her harness off and was comfortably munching her grass, King David sat down to keep watch. The screen of huge boulders, fallen across the front of the cave from the rim above, made a good cover. He was able to see out quite well, but the rocks would block the sight of anyone who might happen to come this way—and the only people likely to be out here were Indians. According to reports he had heard on the wagon train, there were some Indians who were friendly to the settlers, but of course even if he met up with them he had no way to tell them from the hostiles. He had heard that the Brulé Sioux were no danger to the settlers, but there were those who said they were. And then there were always the Piegan and the Pawnee. . . .

King David closed his eyes for a moment as he

slumped behind the screen of boulders, and saw again the horror of the raid: the dead lying where they had fallen, the overturned and burned wagons, household goods smashed and scattered. Rage against the Indians swept over him. We didn't do nothing to them—all we wanted to do was go from a starved-out farm in Missouri to a new chance in Oregon. We was just crossing their country—

Their country. Their country.

The words echoed in his mind as he stared out at the alien land before him, vast and empty and threatening. This is their country. Their country—the Sioux, the Arapaho, the Blackfeet, the Crow, the Cheyenne—like Missouri was *our* country. At least it was when we lived there. What would *we* have done if strange people started coming into Missouri, shooting our cattle to eat, like the settlers shoot buffalo? What would we have done if they had grazed their horses on our grass, pushed us off our land? We would have fought back too, he thought dully. Just like the Sioux. . . .

Oh, Lord, I'm tired. I'm tired of blood and killing, tired of dead men. Just let us git across this country without leaving no more bones out here. Not theirs, not ours. . . .

But how . . . how to cross this wilderness, thread the way through a nation of people who—more than likely with good cause—saw him and Queen of Sheba as enemies?

If only—if *only* Pa was here. If only he had Pa to turn to. Pa always knew what to do. Pa knew about so many things—horses, wagons, people, when to stand and fight, and when to just stand fast to win—

74

King David's head ached, and he could almost smell the blood of the massacre again. His wound, which had eased its paining, started to throb.

"Queen of Sheba," he said abruptly, "I'm going to build a little fire and cook some bacon and make some hot mush." Queen of Sheba looked up hungrily. "And if you promise to be good, I'll get the knife out and whittle on your doll a little bit. I think I can make it look better. And I'll tear this loose strip off the quilt to make a blanket for your doll."

If Queen of Sheba could be kept busy with her doll, she would have less time to cry over icicles . . . to cry for Ma. . . .

11

That night they slept heavily, though once or twice King David awoke to hear the steady rush of the rain across the mouth of the cave and the wind whistling through the broken rocks. At last, his bones aching from the hard earth, he lay awake, staring into the darkness.

His one consuming need was to catch up with the wagons. Everything else was beginning to recede into a fog of lost purposes. He was even—he could now bring himself to acknowledge this—indifferent as to whether they ever made it to Oregon—to the promised land of the Willamette where, he had been told, crops would grow almost overnight and the game was thick in the forests, the rivers full of fish. Maybe later, when they were back with Pa and Ma, and could feel the safety of the wagons and armed men all around them—maybe then he would care again about Oregon. But for now all he wanted was to press on, put one foot in front of the other, make tracks that stitched one horizon to the next and eventually ate up the distance between them and the wagons. He wanted Pa and Ma, a real campfire, hot food, to be able to sleep at night, knowing they were not alone.

He realized that he was far from certain as to the exact whereabouts of the remaining wagons, or how things actually stood with them, although he was sure that they carried wounded, maybe dying, men and women, and had lost horses and cattle, guns and supplies. From the signs he had seen so far, he believed that the raiders had followed the wagons for several days, harrying them and wreaking further damage, although he did not believe any more wagons had been lost.

He could only guess at where they were now and what they were doing, but his best judgment was that they were at least four days ahead of him—a distance of sixty to eighty miles. They were probably near or already at Fort Laramie by now, and he was sure that once the train arrived at the fort, a search party would be sent back to bury the dead and to look for survivors. Wagonmaster Keane and the others would not know that all except him and Queen of Sheba had perished back there at the scene of the first attack. So they would send back a rescue party—and Pa would be with them if he was alive and able to sit on a horse. . . .

The thing that pressed him most at the moment was his lack of surety about directions. He believed he had kept a fairly accurate northwest course after the rain had started and he had lost the trail of the wagons. But it would have been easy for him to have wandered a little to the left or right, and even a small error could put him miles off the trail. As soon as the rain ended he would have to make a big circle around the butte where they were now camped until he cut the wagons' trail again.

Hours crept by, using the day up bit by bit, as the rain continued to fall.

Queen of Sheba had made a bed for her doll. She had arranged a long row of stones, placed a few wisps of grass on them, and now her doll, wrapped in its blanket, lay there.

"This is Margaret Anne Beecham," she told King David, "and she's asleep in the wagon." Queen of Sheba arranged the doll's blanket again, and then went behind a boulder and crouched down out of sight.

As King David watched listlessly, Queen of Sheba reappeared, creeping stealthily around the face of the rock. In her hand was a crooked stick. She slid silently forward, stick upraised. Then, with a shrill cry, she pounced on the doll, whacking and whacking it with the crooked stick.

King David jerked to a horror-struck alertness. Then he lunged forward and raked the stick out of his sister's hand. "What are you doing?" he cried. "You playing—you're an *Indian?*"

Queen of Sheba aimed furious blows at the doll. "I hate her! I hate Margaret Anne Beecham! This is how the Indians do it—I'm going to scalp her—scalp her—scalp her!"

King David stirred the ragged slices of bacon in the little pan. He had built such a small fire that it gave out very little heat, and the bacon was barely cooking. From time to time he glared at Queen of Sheba, who was restlessly arranging and rearranging her doll, but she kept one bony shoulder turned to shut him out of her female business, and her face was granitelike, cold and absorbed.

"You ought to be ashamed," he grunted. "I helped you fix up a nice doll to play with, and then you make out like you're scalping it. You ought to be ashamed. You ain't no Indian."

Carelessly pushing her matted hair back, Queen of Sheba took the doll up and laid it over her shoulder. She was humming tunelessly. "Now it's a baby," she told him grudgingly. "Miz Farrier's baby, Joseph."

"But . . . Miz Farrier's baby . . . died." King David had watched while Pa and some others took shovels to the stony soil, and still others made a tiny coffin. And many had watched while the wagons were driven over the little grave to hide it forever from wolves and other marauders. . . .

"Yes," said Queen of Sheba. "I'm going to bury him in a minute. Dig a grave and bury him."

King David, no longer heated by his anger, shivered. "Why don't you rock the baby," he suggested strongly,

79

"feed it some nice hot mush and rock it to sleep?"

"No. This baby died," said Queen of Sheba. She took up a piece of wood and stubbornly dug a hole and pounded the doll into it. Then she dragged soil up from the floor of the cave and heaped it over to make a grave. "His name is Joseph, and he's dead."

The long afternoon crept by and evening fell, with only the sounds of wind and rain to mark the passing of the hours. King David sat silent, rifle in hand, watching from the front of the cave, even though by now he could see nothing. He had watered the mare from a puddle where water collected as the rain sheeted down the rimrock, and pulled more grass for her. He had been able to refill the canteens with rainwater and then make another flat, greasy mix of cornmeal cooked with water and bacon grease. They both ate a lot—all he had prepared—and he felt comforted a little that his belly no longer hurt.

Before it was completely dark he had cleared the rocks away from a level place on the cave floor, spread the quilt on it, and Queen of Sheba for once crept into it without protest. She lay on her back now, snoring a little, with the doll, which she had dug up from its grave, beside her. Tomorrow, she had told him, the doll would be an Indian, and the soldiers would come and kill him. . . .

12

The rain stopped just before daybreak. King David, sleeping lightly, heard the pounding rush of the rain dwindle and finally cease, but he waited a little longer before crawling out from under the quilt. At the dusky back of the cave, Maggie was sleeping on her feet, her head hanging low, one big hind hoof tilted on its rim. Her harness lay nearby, spread out on a couple of boulders, and the silver balls on the hames gleamed in the dimness.

A pale gray light was creeping in under the overhang by the time King David slid carefully away from Queen of Sheba, so as not to wake her, and stood in the opening behind the big boulders. It was still too dark to see much, but it seemed that the storm was over. Great pearl-colored rifts were appearing in the clouds, and the wind had gentled to become only a fitful breeze. There was a heavy scent of wet earth and sage in the air, and a meadowlark was just beginning to sing.

King David's clothes were still a little damp from the rain, and he would have liked to wrap the quilt around him, but of course he could not do that. He had to leave it tucked around Queen of Sheba to keep her warm. Once again he was swept by a powerful surge of fury and frustration that chance had left her to him to take care of.

It would have been so much easier if he had been left alone, with only himself to feed and shelter. Queen of Sheba was like the loose flap of skin that had been on his wound—he had had to cut it off because of the infection it caused, or it would have killed him. He hoped Queen of Sheba would not prove to be a burden too heavy for him to carry, and cause the death of both of them.

Grudgingly King David left Queen of Sheba asleep and carefully made his way up over the rimrock, where for half an hour he busied himself pulling grass for the mare. The grass was wet but it was better than no feed at all, and the mare seemed to have hollow legs—she ate ravenously all the grass he could gather and then would look around hungrily for more. Even so, she was gaunt. She needed grain to keep up her strength, although they were not really working her that hard.

They had been taking turns riding the horse, although King David's turns had been few and far between. He rode only when his knees threatened to buckle under him, and he was afraid he would collapse and leave Queen of Sheba alone.

Queen of Sheba did not really like riding the mare, and she complained endlessly because Maggie was a workhorse—broad-backed and heavy—and the harness was uncomfortable to sit on. But King David would not take the harness off the horse. He suspected that Maggie was more used to being in harness than to being ridden bareback, and she was flighty enough now, without making her worse. They did indeed look peculiar, journeying along all alone across the prairie with a horse fully harnessed right down to the blinkers on her bridle, and no cart or wagon hitched to her tugs. But peculiar or not, the harness gave him more control over her, and that's what counted most.

After King David fed the horse, he started a very small fire, cooked the last of the bacon and boiled some cornmeal and water. As soon as possible, he put the fire out and fanned the smoke with his coat to disperse it. Although they had not sighted any Indians since the raid, there was no point in taking chances. He still had seven bullets left in the bullet pouch, and enough caps to fire them, but he knew he couldn't load and fire the Sharps fast enough, especially under attack, to do them much good. At best he might get off one, maybe two, good shots. And after that . . .

Queen of Sheba awoke, cranky and peevish. She was very hungry but did not want bacon or boiled cornmeal.

"I want a hot biscuit," she said, "with butter on. And honey—"

"We ain't got none."

"I want fried potatoes."

"We ain't got no potatoes. Eat your bacon and corn-meal."

"Ma don't make me eat no old cornmeal—I want Ma—I want Ma to fix me something to eat—"

King David smothered his exasperation. He was trying—hard—to think, and Queen of Sheba's whining aggravated him till his head started to ache. He couldn't allow anything to distract him—he had to think everything through very carefully, plan their next move. There would be no room for mistakes out here, and no second chances.

On the one hand, they could stay here at the cave, a little safer probably than out on open ground, and try to hold out in case a rescue party came back looking for survivors or maybe another wagon train came through. He had heard that several trains were making the trek this summer, and there was a slight chance that there would be one maybe a few weeks behind theirs, although there was no guarantee that he might be able to sight it from here. The main trail to Oregon was north of them, near the Platte River, but by now he did not know how far away it was. In the meantime, their food supply was dwindling, although they might make it last another three or four days at most. Game was scarce here, mostly antelope that stayed out of range of his rifle, but there was a chance he might be able to shoot some more rabbits.

Equally likely with the arrival of white men, how-ever, was the possibility that Indians might appear. He knew they were all around this territory, and he knew

84

that even though he and Queen of Sheba were hidden in the shallow cave, it wouldn't take Indians long to find them if they should happen to pass this way. For all he knew, the cave might well be a regular stopping place for tribes moving through the area—it had plainly sheltered people many times before this.

Balanced against the possibility of staying in the cave was the possibility of moving out, searching for the tracks of the wagon train, and making a last attempt to either catch up with Pa and Ma and the others or make it alone to Fort Laramie.

He had no illusions about their chances. They were both weak and half starved. Cornmeal and water, even with a little bacon, didn't put much strength into your bones and muscles. He had lost quite a bit of blood, and the fever caused by his wound had weakened him. Queen of Sheba was not a strong child at best—that was one of the reasons why Ma had always favored her so much.

He could see that Queen of Sheba had lost weight these last few days, and even the possibility of getting back to Ma, that he dangled in front of her, barely drove her on. It wasn't impossible that she might just lie down and refuse to move again, and his reduced strength would make it very hard for him to save her then. Given just the right set of conditions, the small package of bone and muscle that made up Queen of Sheba could easily turn into a burden of such intolerable weight that neither of them would live to make it out of this wilderness. . . .

But as the last of the smoke from the little fire drifted away on the breeze, and the sun came out from behind the broken clouds, it seemed that the various possibilities changed into probabilities. The more he thought about it, the more convinced he became that they must go on. Chance of rescue if they waited here was too slim to gamble on. No—they would have to push on—try to make the fort or the wagons before their last supplies of food and ammunition and their remaining strength gave out.

King David forced Queen of Sheba to choke down a few bites of the soggy cornmeal and then ate all she left. He harnessed Maggie and led her out from under the overhang and then boosted Queen of Sheba up onto her broad back. With some regret, he looked back once into the shelter of the cave and then led Maggie down the slope, in what he hoped would be the right direction.

By late morning, they were no more than five or six miles from the cave. King David had realized that he must make every effort to locate the tracks of the wagon train because they could not afford to waste time going the wrong way. As the sky cleared, he quickly got his directions from the sun, and he knew that the wagons had to be moving toward the north-west.

Accordingly, when they set out, he had set for his course a half circle, hoping to cut across the track and follow it in. The farther west they traveled, the more broken the country became, slowly rising, he supposed, into the higher country that flanked the massive ranges of the Rocky Mountains ahead. With the rain over, the wet ground would dry fast, and he was fairly sure that the tracks of the wagons would still be visible enough to follow.

Queen of Sheba bobbed along on the horse without saying much. Her face was drawn, and her silence made him nervous.

"Look, Queen of Sheba," he tried to arouse her, "way over there—some antelope. Sure wish I could shoot one. Then we'd eat good."

"I'm hungry," the child said listlessly.

"I know. When we catch up with the wagons you'll have something good to eat. Biscuits and honey, maybe, or beans—"

"My legs hurt."

He paused to look where she pointed and was dismayed at the sight. Both of her bony legs were bruised and raw where the horse's harness rubbed the skin as she rode. No wonder she complained so much about riding the mare. Maybe if he let her walk awhile she would hush up about that one misery at least.

"All right," he said, lifting her down. "I'll let you walk awhile. Why don't you eat an apple? We still got some left."

Queen of Sheba accepted an apple and settled into a shuffling walk. King David had tied the strings of her sunbonnet under her chin to protect her face from the sun and keep the heat from tiring her as long as possible. Her shoes, he noted, were beginning to show heavy wear from the stony ground and abrasive sand; the toes were scuffed and a button was missing from the left one. Margaret Anne Beecham's pa might have more money than Pa, but he didn't buy very good shoes for his daughter.

King David took one of the remaining apples and climbed onto the horse. Maggie snorted and raised a foot to kick, but as soon as he was astride she settled into her usual plodding walk.

As they pushed ahead, the land was becoming rougher, with low rocky ridges and shallow swales, and a dry stream bed, that made it hard to see very far in any direction. Once he got off and left the mare, with Queen of Sheba holding the rope, standing just under the crest of a hill so he could go forward and reconnoiter without exposing them to view.

Luke Skinner's hat was so big on him that he had to tilt his head far back to see out from under the brim. Queen of Sheba stared at him. "Why don't you take that hat off?" she muttered. "You look silly."

"Can't do that," he told her. "A hawk just flew by, and if she looked down and saw this hole in my head, she might think it looked like a hole in a hollow tree and decide to build a nest in it. And what would I do with baby birds hatching out inside my head?" Queen of Sheba only stared silently at him.

"Well, come on," he said flatly. "Let's git moving. I'll ride the horse—you can walk if you'd rather, but keep close behind me, now—"

It was past the middle of the afternoon when King David's eyes, blurring again with fatigue, picked out a faint mark across the next grassy hill. Eagerly he pressed forward, pushing the mare along. Yes—there was another mark farther on. Wagon tracks—no doubt about it—wagon tracks! He jerked the mare to a halt and slid off to peer closely at the crushed grass.

"It's their tracks!" he called excitedly over his shoulder to Queen of Sheba. "We done it! Now all we got to do is follow their tracks!"

Filled once more with hope and energy, he climbed back onto the mare and kicked her sides to get her moving as fast as possible. "Come on—walk as fast as you can. Let's see how far we can go before dark—"

His head was pounding again, but King David pushed forward. Sighting the wagon tracks had flooded him with optimism. He could believe once more that they would make it now—yes, they would make it now.

He did not know how much time had gone by since they struck the trail of the wagons, but suddenly the leveling rays of the sun made King David look up from the wagon tracks. The tired mare thudded to a stop, lowered her head, snorted up a puff of dust from the ground, and grabbed a mouthful of the scanty grass that grew among the red and yellow flowering prickly pears. They had just crossed a low rise and were dropping down into a swale where clumps of tall sage were clustered.

"Guess we'll take cover in that high brush over there," said King David as he slid off the mare. "Be dark soon. Got to eat a little, get some sleep. You tired, Queen of Sheba?"

He looked around, expecting a peevish reply from

the child. But behind the horse lay only an empty reach of grass and stunted sage, spotted here and there with buffalo wallows. All he could see were the horse's tracks. Nothing more.

Queen of Sheba was gone.

13

King David stared, stupefied, at the horse, the empty wasteland, the flaming sunset sky.

"Queen of Sheba!" he shouted. "Where are—hey! Answer me—Queen of Sheba—"

He grabbed the mare's lead rope and whirled her around, scrambled up onto her back. With the end of the rope he flogged her sides. Snorting and bucking, Maggie lunged to throw him off, and it was all he could do to hold on—he would have lost her if he hadn't had the harness to grab.

He lashed the mare again and again, and finally she lowered her head, broke into a shambling trot back the way they had come. King David's eyes raked the flank of every low hill, searched the draws and the skyline for a sight of the child. Nothing met his eyes but dry wastes, cactus, grass, sage, rocks.

He had pushed perhaps a mile back down their trail when the mare, sweating and winded, balked again. King David slid off her and led her forward more slowly, his eyes searching for tracks. Trouble was, Queen of Sheba was so small, she hadn't enough weight to make a heavy track. Unless he found a place where she had crossed bare earth, it would be very hard to find the track of her shoes.

The sun set and still he pushed on, cursing Queen of Sheba for being contrary, for getting lost, and himself for being stupid, careless. I wasn't thinking, he told himself. I knew she was tired and cranky—why didn't I watch her closer? Just because I know enough to keep on going don't mean she does. She's bad-tempered anyhow—I can't count on her doing things just because I tell her to. Pa—Pa would have been watching her—*he* wouldn't never forget—Pa—oh, God, why couldn't I do like Pa would have done?

When his legs began to tremble, King David halted for a moment. Before him lay only empty land, darkening now as the sun dropped below the horizon, with blue gray shadows filling the dips and hollows. It was already getting hard to see marks in the dusty ground. He had been backtracking Maggie's hoof prints—surely Queen of Sheba would have just got mad and thrown herself down where she stood beside their own trail. But suppose she had wandered off to one side or the other—hiding from him, looking for wild flowers, or following a pretty bird?

Slowly the futility of his situation began to creep over

him with the gathering dark. The country was as vast, as empty, as the moon itself, and Queen of Sheba was so very small. If she chose to hide from him because she was tired of walking and riding, or simply lay down to sleep, he could pass within a few yards of her and not see her. And with darkness coming on—

King David halted and Maggie thudded to a stop. He turned and leaned against the horse, his face pressed to her smooth, satiny neck. It was hopeless to go on. There was nothing to do now but wait out the night right here. Moving on in the dark, he would run the risk of losing the trail, and he had sense enough left to know that he had better not do that. He had only so much strength left in him, and wasting it wandering aimlessly around on the prairie would not save either of them.

At last, he tied the mare's rope around his ankle, for lack of even a stout bush to tether her to, and wrapped the quilt around him. He checked the rifle—it was loaded except for a cap—and lay down with both hands clenched around it. As he fell into an exhausted sleep, King David kept seeing Ma's and Pa's faces, kept seeing himself trying to explain to them how he had lost Queen of Sheba.

It was very cold when he awoke. The first rays of the sun were turning the endless reaches of sand and thin grass to a copper color beneath the pale blue of the sky, and a meadowlark skimming by overhead sent a trill of music spilling down over him. He had been dreaming and for a few seconds more he thought he must be back in his rope bed, in the loft of the old cabin in Missouri, with Ma downstairs cooking up some hot mush for breakfast and Pa shouting for him to get to the milking, feed the calves, and start hoeing the weeds that daily threatened to starve out the corn patch.

Yes, Pa . . . for as long as he could remember, Pa had been there, telling him what to do, holding him responsible for one thing or another. King David had grown up with Pa's big shadow blotting out the sun and sky; sometimes he had wanted to get out of that shadow, find out if he himself had a shadow. . . .

But when he opened his eyes, the dream and the shadow were gone, and all he could see was the gray earth beneath him, a clump of cactus three feet away, and beyond that—empty prairie. A wave of despair swept over him, and he clenched his eyes shut. It would have been better to have stayed in Missouri. At least there had been someone to talk to, someone to tell him what to do. . . .

There was a sharp, painful tug on his ankle, and he was forced to open his eyes, look up. Well, here was someone telling him what to do—the mare wanted feed and water. He wondered dully if he had strength enough to get onto his feet, search for a gully where there might be a puddle of water left from the storm.

The mare pawed the ground restlessly. Slowly, King David climbed to his feet. His fingers fumbled as he reassembled the pack and strapped it to Maggie's back. He made himself choke down a few mouthfuls of corn-meal, had a sip of water from the canteen. Ahead of them lay a patch of dry grass, and he led Maggie to it, sat down on the ground, and let her graze.

It took a long time for the mare to crop enough of the short dry grass so that he felt he could start on. At last he got to his feet, gave the halter rope a tug, and they set out again, with Maggie still chewing on a wisp of grass.

But now with each passing moment King David became more hopeless. Throughout the whole long ordeal, until Queen of Sheba had disappeared, he at least had the feeling that they were moving forward—that if they just kept dragging one foot after the other, sooner or later they would either catch up with the wagons or reach the fort.

But now he had turned around and was going backward—into danger, starvation, exhaustion, death. All the effort he had made so far was now being wiped out just because Queen of Sheba was gone. It only galled him worse knowing that this need not have happened. He had realized that she was very tired, but if she could not walk any farther, she had only to tell him, and he would have put her back on the horse. Up till now, she had kept up a steady grumble—why, oh, *why* had she not yelled at him, hollered, threatened to tell Ma that he was being mean to her—this time? It might have saved them both. Once again the specter of Pa rose up before him. Pa would have known better than to turn his back on Queen of Sheba. He would have known she couldn't keep up. . . . would have set himself, as he always did, to fight for the weak ones—

Toward noon, with the sun hot on his shoulders and his eyes squinting from straining to see the far reaches of the prairie, he pulled the mare to a halt. He tried to sit in her shadow for a little relief, but she was cranky and threatened to kick and bite. In the end, he just sank down there in the blazing sun and rested his head on his arms.

In the blackness behind his closed eyes, he now began to see fanciful scenes—Ma and Pa and the team and wagon, the train halted for nooning, or circled at night. The herds of cattle and extra horses. Campfires and cooking pots. And the fort—somewhere ahead on the trail—the fort with its food, its water, its walls, its soldiers. Its safety.

Why am I doing this? Completely unbidden, the thought crept into his exhausted mind. She's gone. For whatever reason, Queen of Sheba is gone. I ain't never going to find her. All I'm going to do is kill myself looking for her. God Almighty, do You expect me to kill myself too? I tried to save her. She ain't easy to take care of, but I tried as hard as I could. It ain't my fault—

He must have fallen asleep for a while, because the next thing he knew he was lying on the ground with the rough grass pricking his cheek. He sat up stiffly, rubbing his left arm, which he had lain on, to drive out the stiffness. The mare was dozing on her feet, switching her tail to drive away insects. A faint breeze was blowing, but it carried only the smell of dry grass and stony ground. No sound broke the stillness but the songs of insects buzzing in the hot air and the cry of a hawk wheeling far above in the empty sky.

King David crawled to his feet. He was weak from hunger, his head throbbed, his legs would barely hold him. There was a singing sound in his ears.

"Maggie." He spoke aloud and then was startled at

the sound of his own voice. He looked around as if expecting to see someone, but the slopes of the low hills, the farthest reaches he could see, were empty, sunburned, silent.

"Git up, Maggie." King David drew a deep breath. "I can't go back no farther. Queen of Sheba's lost. It ain't my fault. Pa—I got to make him see that. It ain't my fault. I'm going—on—after the wagons—"

I'll think of something to tell Pa. And Ma. They ain't here. They won't know—nobody will ever know—I quit looking for her—

14

As he had expected, Maggie went forward better when he turned her around. Her harness jingled softly and her gait freshened. He knew that her sure instinct told her that once again they were on the way to safety, to feed and water, to the company of other horses and men.

King David forced himself to eat a few mouthfuls of cornmeal as he walked just ahead of the horse, but it was hard to get them down dry. There was only a little water left in one canteen, and the other was empty. Earlier, he had counted on reaching a low outcrop of hills to the northwest, where he hoped there might be springs. but going back to search for Queen of Sheba had used up too much time. The water was almost gone, and without water he would soon die—

A wind came up in the afternoon that bedeviled him with whirls and puffs of dust that blinded him, making him stumble into clumps of prickly pears and their sharp, gouging thorns. Once or twice he wandered off the trail—it wasn't all that clear—and only his sharp memory, identifying this rock, that clump of grass, pulled him back.

But aside from the hunger in his belly and his dry mouth, that felt like the dust under his feet, there was the other, much worse, torture. It rode his back like an iron demon, and with every step he took it weighed him down. How can I make Ma and Pa understand? They weren't out here—alone—scared of Indians— scared of starving to death. I got to make them understand that it wasn't my fault. I did the best I could—

It was late afternoon and the sun was slipping low in a burning, cloudless sky, when a tickle of memory began to stir in the back of his head. For no reason at all that he could think of, he began to see pictures of Queen of Sheba when they were back at the stream. Queen of Sheba playing in the water. Queen of Sheba making mud pies. Queen of Sheba wading, shoes in her hand. So far as he knew, Queen of Sheba loved just two things—Ma, and playing in water. Ma used to fix a big pan of water for Queen of Sheba, and the child would play around it all afternoon, contented as a duck. Yes, water drew Queen of Sheba like a magnet. Pa used to laugh and say that she could locate water better than a diviner, and if there was any around you would find her there. Yes, Pa used to say that a lot—

King David stopped. He stared down at the hard, dry earth beneath his feet. Maggie snorted up dust and kicked restlessly. She was hungry and thirsty too—had been without water all day.

Something stirred in King David's mind. A shadow, a dream. A memory. Pa, did I miss—something?

And without knowing what he was really doing, without a clear plan or even a good look at the encircling, empty land, he pulled Maggie around once more, to backtrack. There had to be something there—something he had missed the first time.

An hour passed, and with darkness coming on he began to lose track of his thoughts, time, even their passage over the desolate, stony waste. But now he forced himself to look for something different. He forced himself to scan every draw and hollow for the merest hint of green. A clump of grass, a tuft of leaves. Anything.

And found it. Off there to the right. So small, so far away—no wonder he had not seen it before. Barely visible above the crest of a low intervening ridge was a slender line of something green. Trees?

Eagerly he turned Maggie aside and headed toward it. Maggie balked and shuffled, but he drove her forward. At first it did not seem possible—how could he have missed the presence of water anywhere near when they needed it so badly?

But when they crested the hill, a silent shout went up in him. There it was—a slender, slender thread of green. A little grass, a few willows—one or two tiny pools. Water! It was a spring, replenished and running from the recent rainstorms. Small, scanty, but oh, so precious.

Maggie broke into a stumbling trot and then a gallop. He could not have stopped her if he had wanted to, but he knew he could catch up when they got to the spring.

The horse plunged down the slope, sliding and rattling small rocks under her hooves, to sink her muzzle into the first tiny basin of water. She did not raise it till the pool was dry.

King David threw himself down to drink and gulped up water till he thought he would burst. Then he quickly scrambled back to the horse, grabbed a canteen, and managed to fill it before Maggie, her own pool dry, impatiently thrust him aside and drained the second. At last, filled and contented, she raised her head, chewing and flapping loose lips, to look around her. She sighted a patch of green grass growing along the bottom of the draw beside the stunted willows and immediately shambled over to it and began to graze.

King David sat for a while in a daze. He had no clear memory of the last few hours, but somehow they had found water—water that he had missed the first time. Whether or not Queen of Sheba had actually found this place, he could not guess, but he himself certainly would not have found it if he had not turned back the second time.

After a few moments' rest, he located a smooth spot to lay the pack and where he could sleep. As he ate some cornmeal—it was getting very low—he tried to figure out which was more important—finding feed for the horse and water for both of them, or the fact that he had lost so much time and still might never be able to find Queen of Sheba after all. But he was tired, clear through to the marrow of his bones, and there was no use even thinking about it anymore. Sleep. He needed sleep. . . .

It was very dark now, and great flaming white stars were coming out in the black sky. The night wind whispered softly through the willows, and an owl of some kind went by overhead with a soft rushing of wings. He tethered Maggie to a sturdy willow tree, unrolled the quilt, and rechecked the rifle. He felt he was as secure as he could be under the circumstances.

Just before the last of the light went, King David decided to walk a few yards down the draw and see how far the surface water went. Maybe there were a few more pools—he might find enough to water the mare in the morning and fill the other canteen.

As he stepped carefully down the draw from rock to rock, he could see very little. A pale patch ahead there was probably a clump of sunflowers—that over there would be a white stone—

His foot came down on something softer than a rock, firm, but softer. He halted, stepped back. Curious, he bent to feel around, pick up the object he had stepped on.

And although he now could see almost nothing, he didn't need to see to know what he held in his hand.

A shoe.

Queen of Sheba's shoe.

And the second one lay only a foot away.

In the darkness King David stood still, feeling the night wind wash over him. *I was right. She did see the trees—she knew there was water where there were green trees.* Queen of Sheba left the trail, left off following him and Maggie, turned aside, came here looking for water. She's here—or *was* here—someplace. Maybe not too far away—

"Queen of Sheba! Queen of Sheba! Where are you— answer me—Queen of Sheba!" He shouted and shouted again, using all the strength in him and pushing out every bit of sound he could make. "Queen of Sheba! Where are you? Answer me—Queen of Sheba—"

But the sound of his voice seemed to soak into the darkness and just vanish. There was no answer—no fretful, peevish little girl voice coming back to him from out of the vast black night. At last he stopped shouting. No use. She must be out of earshot. Maybe asleep. Yes, probably asleep by this time of night. And if she was, she would probably sleep till daylight. And when daylight came, he would be on his feet, rested, ready to go on—

With one of Queen of Sheba's shoes in each hand, he turned back to his camp. And for the first time in his life, he thanked God that Queen of Sheba hated shoes, took them off whenever she could. And dropped them where she was standing . . .

15

It was the longest night he had ever lived through. He slept hardly at all—dozing briefly and then starting up at every tiny sound: a puff of wind, the stamp of Maggie's hooves, the call of a coyote. His mind was so active, it was like a nest of mice inside his head, with ideas jumping and leaping in all directions.

Doubts tormented him. Was Queen of Sheba still here—would he find her—and then if he found her, did they have enough food and strength to keep them going till they could make it back to the track of the wagon train? And then follow after the train, maybe even as far as Fort Laramie itself? More time had been lost, and they had only so much time. . . .

Long before daybreak, he was awake. He heard

Maggie grazing comfortably, and he got up once to see if the little pools had again filled with water. They had risen a few inches. Not enough to fill the canteens, but enough to give him and the horse a drink to start with. And maybe there was more water farther down the draw.

When it was barely daylight he untied the horse, led her to the spring, and let her drink. He drank too, although Maggie had stirred up the water and it had sand and mosses in it. At last they were as ready as they ever would be. King David decided not to eat anything—the supply of cornmeal was now very low—but just to push on and see what the day brought.

He had examined the shoes carefully in the first light to make certain they were the ones Queen of Sheba had been wearing. But he knew they were—they were perfectly familiar from the scuffed toes and scratched soles to the missing button on the left one. He placed the shoes inside his shirt, like a talisman, and led Maggie away down the draw.

The sun rose and the air began to lose its early morning chill. At times the pools of water petered out as they went forward, and there was no single blade of grass or willow tree. Then he would round a bend in the ravine and find a thread of water, a tiny patch of shade in a clump of stubby willows. Once he was able to scoop a cup or two of water into one of the canteens.

But with every passing moment, he was getting farther from the wagon track. How long could he go on? How long could he risk going on with the search?

An hour had passed and the sun was hot as he led

Maggie around a sharp bend. Ahead he could see that the draw looked more open, and a clump of willows thrust up green and inviting. He yanked on Maggie's rope, stumbled around an outcrop of rocks—

And saw her.

16

Queen of Sheba was crouched over a tiny pool. She sat on the muddy ground, bent forward, staring down at the trickle of water. Her sunbonnet hung down her back, and her face was blistered by the sun. Listlessly she patted the mud with one hand and leaned on the other. She was making mud pies.

King David sucked in a deep breath, ready to shout her name, scream, or cry. And suddenly stopped.

There was another child beside the pool. Behind Queen of Sheba on the other side of the water hole sat a small brown boy, nearly naked, with jet black hair hanging down his back. His skin was coppery brown, his face broad, and he crouched there silent as a rabbit, silent as a stone, watching Queen of Sheba. An Indian boy.

Go get her—a voice shouted noiselessly in King David's head—go get her and get away from here—*fast*—

But as he stepped forward, someone else stepped forward out of the willows.

It was an Indian woman. She had a basket in one hand and a knife in the other—she must have been gathering roots.

The Indian woman took in the scene much faster than he had—saw him, King David, there fifty feet away, weary, swaying, even saw that he carried the rifle muzzle down at his side. She dropped her basket and stepped forward, seized Queen of Sheba by the arm, and dragged her up. Queen of Sheba looked up wildly, and a tiny cry sounded across the glade.

The Indian woman glared at King David defiantly. Steal—he could read her mind clear across the hot, grass-scented swale. I'll steal this child—steal this child with the golden hair—

But he could not let the woman do that. Even as he raised the rifle, fumbled a cap into place, he told himself that he could not let Queen of Sheba disappear from his sight ever again.

The Indian woman had courage. As he leveled the rifle, aimed at the breast of her fringed and beaded skin dress, she faced him without flinching, her eyes black and bright above the two vermillion circles on her cheeks. And slowly she brought her knife up to Queen of Sheba's throat.

Without a sound, King David slowly swung the barrel of the rifle till it was sighted on the Indian child.

A moment passed. Another.

King David began to hear a ringing in his ears—he was very tired—and it got louder and louder as he sighted down the long barrel of the Sharps. With the cruel lessons of the massacre branded on his mind, he could almost smell the blood—knew what the sound would be—how that small body would jerk and fling and explode if he pulled the trigger—

"Kill them!" screamed Queen of Sheba.

There was a roaring in his head. Pa—what shall I do?

"King David—shoot—" Queen of Sheba's voice was shrill, terrified. Her face was almost unrecognizable. But Pa would know her—Pa knew everything—Pa—knew when to shoot—when to bluff—when to move and when to wait—

I got to *win* here, he told himself. Pa would win—*I got to win*—

Slowly, slowly, King David lowered the barrel of the gun. Lowered it till it pointed harmlessly at the ground. Gambling, he said to himself. I'm gambling with Queen of Sheba's life. But I can either tell Pa I killed an Indian and lost Queen of Sheba—or—

Moving as if her arm had frozen, the Indian woman slowly opened her fingers, released Queen of Sheba.

As if shot from a bow, Queen of Sheba sprang forward, raced up the slope, shrieking, "Kill them—kill them—"

King David let Queen of Sheba run past him. He held the rifle ready, but down a little.

Silently, her eyes on King David's face, the Indian woman reached for her child. She seized his arm and turned him, led him through the willows. Then she grabbed him and started to scramble up the far slope of the ravine.

King David grabbed Queen of Sheba with one hand and Maggie's rope with the other and started to run.

17

The cornmeal was completely gone. King David had turned the bag inside out to get the very last crumbs, dribbling them carefully into Queen of Sheba's little hand so she could lick them up. She ate them hungrily without complaining. Sitting close to her, he could see the deep hollows in her neck and cheeks, the thinness of her arms and legs, the blue shadows under her eyes. Days of hunger, of walking endless mile after endless mile, nights sleeping on the cold, hard ground, had taken a heavy toll of her. She seemed fragile, brittle, like a child made out of dry twigs.

"Why don't you throw away that old piece of wood," he said. "It ain't really a doll, and it's too heavy for you to carry."

Queen of Sheba roused briefly. She raised the lumpy

111

wooden form and laid it over her shoulder, patting her hand on its back. "No!" she said with faint defiance. "This is my baby. My little girl. She's mine and I love her. I got to tell Margaret Anne Beecham how I saved her from the Indians."

King David stared in surprise. A few days ago she had planned to scalp the doll, and then it had been a corpse to be buried. Puzzled, but with understanding beginning, like a seed, to sprout and grow, he muttered in wonder, "All . . . in what she sees. All in what she sees—"

At last, King David stood up and looked around. He figured they had probably covered four or five miles from the place where he had found Queen of Sheba with the Indians; and now, after a short rest, it was time to press on. He guessed that the Indian woman had done nothing to sound an alarm, since there had been no pursuit.

Maybe she, too, knew that she had to win. He and Queen of Sheba would both be dead now, King David thought, if he had fired so much as a single shot back there at the water hole. I got to tell Pa, he thought wearily. I got to tell Pa about not shooting the Indian boy—about how both me and the Indian woman *won*, like Queen of Sheba's got to tell Margaret Anne Beecham about the doll. . . .

With great effort he picked Queen of Sheba up and sat her on the horse. No more could he trust her to follow, or ever let his attention wander from her for more than a moment. It was clear to him that they were now making their last effort, and whatever his feelings about his sister had been yesterday, today he

112

knew that they would make it together, or not at all.

He had tried his best to figure out what to do. With time running out on them, he could not afford to waste one step, one minute, and that meant that he had not been able to backtrack yesterday's trail to where he had turned off to find Queen of Sheba. Instead they must lay a diagonal course to try to bring them back to the point where he had discovered the child's absence. That would bring them back to the wagon track, and the only hope they had.

Now with the noon sun high behind them and slowly coming around to where it beat on the sides of their faces, King David sighted across the land in the direction they must go. He carried the Sharps, loaded, in one hand so as to be ready for anything that might happen, even though its weight strained the weakened muscles of his arm.

Queen of Sheba rode, swaying to the horse's gait, sometimes quiet and sometimes talking to herself. "Margaret Anne Beecham," he heard her mutter once, "Margaret Anne Beecham—"

After about two hours of travel he halted the horse and lifted Queen of Sheba down; and after drinking the last of the water, they sat for some time, resting and simply staring off toward the horizon. An idle wind drifted over the empty wasteland, and heat shimmered in the distance. Ranges of hills were rising ahead now, and their blue flanks looked cool and remote. King David wondered if they would make it to the hills. He wondered too why he had tried so hard to save himself and Queen of Sheba, against such hopeless odds. Why had he gone back for Queen of Sheba?

113

Pa . . . he'd know. Pa . . . he knows everything. I'll have to ask Pa . . . why I went back. . . .

Queen of Sheba stirred. "Are we almost there, King David?" Her eyes were sunken, but still she held the doll against her breast.

"Almost there," promised King David. "Almost there."

"I got to show Margaret Anne Beecham my doll. And tell her—how we rescued it from the Indians."

"Yeah. We'll tell her. Come on. We got to git started."

With arms that trembled he lifted Queen of Sheba and got her back onto the horse. Got to keep moving. Got to keep moving. As the horse settled into her shuffling gait, it seemed that the creak and jingle of her harness made a sound—got to keep moving. Got to keep moving. . . .

In the late afternoon, he began to know that they could not go on much longer. Even the fact that his plan had worked and they had now struck the wagon trail again did not seem very important. Hunger was tearing a hole in him, and his legs were like wet straw, ready to fold at every step. Food—food—if only they had something to eat—

And then—incredibly—he saw a rabbit. It was a big one, loping slowly up the rise to his left.

Without a moment's thought about scaring the horse, frantic to secure food before they both starved, King David slipped a cap out of the box and onto the nipple of the Sharps, raised it to aim. The gun trembled in his weak arms—he sighted—fired—and the

114

rabbit dropped over. "I got him! I got him!" he cried.

Behind him Maggie squealed and reared. In a moment Queen of Sheba, too weak to hold onto the harness, slipped off the horse and crashed to the ground. Maggie threw up her head and broke into a stumbling gallop. With the smoking rifle still raised, King David watched paralyzed as the horse charged up the slope ahead of them.

Frantically he ran back to Queen of Sheba, seized her arm, dragged her up. She was dazed and bleeding from a cut on her face, but still she clung to the doll.

"Get up—" he gasped, "I'll get the rabbit—in a minute—help me—catch the horse! You head her off to the right—"

But Maggie had suddenly lurched to a halt, her harness creaking and the halter rope blowing back in the wind. She stood on the crest of the hill head up, tail flying. Her ears were pricked forward.

Then she whinnied.

King David froze. That meant Maggie had sighted other horses—

He pushed Queen of Sheba down. "Stay here. I got to—go see—may be—Indians—"

With the rifle up, his breath burning in his chest, he stumbled forward, fumbling for a cap. He had only a few balls left—

Suddenly dark shapes pricked the skyline over the crest of the hill—horses—horses—

King David's ears caught the jingle of bridle bits—the creak of saddles—a shouted word—

Three men rode over the crest of the hill.

The rider in the lead—his face half covered with bandages and one arm in a sling—was Pa.

And when he saw Pa there—tall on a tall black horse—King David knew why he had gone back to save Queen of Sheba.